Also by Donald S. Olson

The Secrets of
MABEL EASTLAKE

PARADISE GARDENS

DONALD S. OLSON

Knights
Press

Stamford, Connecticut

Cover design by Gary H. Larson ©

Published by Knights Press, P.O. Box 454, Pound Ridge, NY 10576

Distributed by Lyle Stuart, Inc.

Library of Congress Cataloging-in-Publication Data

Olson, Donald S.
    Paradise Gardens

    I. Title.
PS3565.L825P3   1988   813'.54   87-37939
ISBN 0-915175-26-6 (pbk.)

Printed in the United States of America

FOR

Gary H. Larson

PARADISE GARDENS

Late Summer

1981

High stone walls surround the house and property. From the street, only the second story of the old brick house can be seen, its tiled roof falling in orderly waves down to the gutters. Every year, under the eaves, an ancient, agile wisteria vine blossoms and makes the upper story look as though it had been scribbled purple. Looking out from those second floor windows late in the spring, only the sweet dripping flower clusters are seen, singing with bees.

The front of the house, although partially hidden by the wall, presents itself like a perfect host to a waiting public. Everything is in order. The grass is always cut. The bushes of camellia, azalea, andromeda and spirea stand at clipped, tidy attention. The windows stare clean. Like every other house in the old, well-kept neighborhood by the river, this one breathes an air of security and high taxes. The roots of the great horse-chestnut trees on either side of it have had time to sink very deep.

The high stone walls turn back and proceed to enclose, you think, a diligent, predictable oblong box of land in which the house should sit like a square, geometrical fetus. But this does not happen. Unseen from the street, the walls begin to fan out, widen, as if pressure from the very space they are enclosing is forcing them to expand. They encompass two acres of land and end without joining at a cold, deep river. Willows, like arboreal forms of water, whisper in a long row on the river's raised bank.

Time is a slow but constant preoccupation in the mind of a gardener. Time is planting, growth, color and fruit—the progressing pulse of the soil and what is in it. When the walls were first erected, trees were planted within their periphery, and there they stand now, in back of the house, hiding much of the stone, stretching into space to form themselves luxuriantly, without cramp, in the freedom of the air. There are giant blue spruce, nodding in the wind; white birch, dreamily ejaculating their yellow seeds in April; immense poplars, stark as picked skeletons in winter, but green and flexible in summer. There are old, experienced apple trees and more horsechestnuts, laden with candles in May and hurling down barbaric-looking nuts in the fall. Maples, mountain ash, lilac and azalea. Rhododendrons which have gone home in spirit to the valleys of the Himalayas, where they were first found.

And now the inner garden, a dense vortex of flowers, herbs and vegetables spinning off into those taller certainties of trees and shrubs closer to the walls. This inner garden is hidden from the curious eye: a mysterious heart full of palpitations, scented breathing, rhythms of fertility and language of form. It is the beating heart in whose chambers life and death live together, where meaning flames on a stalk, visible, and the eye is haunted by a pageant of beauty so ancient and so intense that it can be as much sorrow as joy to see it.

Birds flash in and out from dark leafy branches, nesting, resting, singing. Cats arrange themselves like carved ornaments on the shadowy coping, watching the birds. Spiders spin the complicated designs of their survival; flies, gnats, fat bees and tiresome wasps work and buzz, to be gobbled by the birds and caught by the spiders.

It is summer . . . but unmoored autumn drifts slowly in the currents of hot sparkling air. It is morning, but afternoon is wading into the freshness of the sky. The air is dry but waiting to turn giddy, waiting for change. A thin staring sky rolls its faded blue high and flat above. Stillness. Quiet, except for a fountain's murmur. Worm-fat robins perch in the crown of a tree, dangling apples ripening around them.

These are the Paradise Gardens.

A head of thin, dark hair neatly combed. A man. Tortoise-shell glasses slightly magnify his dark, swollen eyes. Age has defined his face, rid it of superfluity. A prominent nose subject for years to the poltergeists of pollen. Lips thin and habitually compressed. A direct, dignified face.

Khaki trousers; a pale shirt open at the neck; dark, polished oxfords. He walks slowly, almost shuffling . . . stops and clutches a box to his chest. Sneezes.

There is a direct path from the back terrace of the house to the bluestone steps that descend to the river. Myriad gravel and grass walks radiate from the central path to other parts of the garden. Holding the box, the man proceeds along the central path until he is midway between house and river.

Here is the center of the garden, with its weight of silent secrecy. The gravel path ends at a large simple grassy circle surrounded by a high laurel hedge cut with six openings. In the center, there is a small stone pool and, on a pedestal above it, a smaller than life-sized statue: bearded, togaed, holding a spade in one hand. The other hand is mossy and extended: feeling for rain? pointing to the sun? proclaiming to Nature? wafting magic through the six openings in the laurel hedge? From a spout below his toes a thread of water splashes into the basin.

The man stops and looks solemnly into the pool, where orange and black carp glide twilight-cool among waterlilies. His face suddenly contorts and he sneezes again. He wipes his nose, dabs his eyes and forehead with a handkerchief, never relinquishing the small box. Sniffing, looking tenderly at the box, he leaves the pool and takes another path through the laurel hedge.

Thickly mysterious where he enters. Sun and deep shadows cast, withdraw. There is repose here, deep abiding quiet. The man with the small box held to his heart stops in the path, snagged like a wandering dream. He walks on, slowly, his eyes searching along the peripheries of the overgrown path. He peers among the lowest, largest leaves. Then he sees what he is looking for, and again his face changes. Tears drip regular, hot, and his lips twitch, holding back a wordless grief.

Near an old chosen rose there is a simple marker. His long clean scholar's fingers dig near it, under the rose. The soil is rich, earth-cool, loamy. Scents sing old mourning melodies in his wet nose; he sniffs them up with the mucus. When he opens his mouth to suck in a breath, the air tastes warm, pungent, full.

Herbs grow all around—he cannot name them and this adds to his sorrow. Flowers watch, wait. He feels a root of the rose as he digs, its subterranean skeleton, and he thinks instantly of death, of the network of being that lies beneath life, of the possible nothingness there.

The closest we come to knowing death is by not remembering our dreams, those stylized germinations of what has happened to us and what will never happen to us. We grow, flower, and in the end spit the seed of our life—spit all that we have been—into a great still wind of unknowing. While we live we may think that this seed of ourselves will find soil and germinate in a clear new ground where we will grow and flower forever. For mortal man, that is paradise. But death comes first, to puzzle and make us mourn our uncertainties, our unknowing.

With fumbling soiled fingers the small box is opened. The man looks into it, swallowing hard, sniffling, his eyes dimmed with dripping tears. "Just cry," he tells himself. "Just go ahead and cry, goddamn it."

Carefully he sets the box down and reaches for his hand-kerchief, blowing, wiping. Glasses removed, he wipes his red eyes and wet cheeks. Again he holds the box, lifts it as a priest might lift an offering to the gods. He seems about to say something, looks up to the sky, blinks in the sun.

There is nothing to say.

Quickly he pours the ashes from the box into the hole he has dug.

Now, crouched on his knees, he looks into the empty box and then sits back, taking deep ragged breaths. One hand goes out to the hole filled with ashes. The man looks hard, hard, attempting to scrutinize something more closely than he ever has in his life—some great mystery hidden there, mute, before him.

He peers at a smudge of ash on his finger, his face fills with pain, and he puts the finger slowly into his mouth. The tears drip faster and faster, his body rocks, and finally his grief explodes like a giant flower that can blossom only once before dying.

Deep jagged sounds rise from his deepest parts. His hands crumble and clutch the cool earth. Unconnected and strange, he dimly hears a robin shrilling in a nearby pine tree. One of the first ripe apples falls with a muffled crash into the laurel.

Spring, Summer

1971

They were expected to sit in absolute silence while Birgit Nilsson sang *"Ozean, Du Ungeheuer"* from Weber's opera *Oberon*.

Professor Francis Turner, whose house they were in, listened with his face held taut and stiffly attentive. With his thin hands folded in his lap, shoes touching, bony ankles exposed, eyelids closed but quivering, his was an altogether meticulously ecstatic posture.

Professor Turner held one prim corner of a long leather sofa. At the other end sprawled his long-time platonic friend, Dobbin Riggs. Unlike Francis Turner, with his baggy English gray woolen suit, Dobbin Riggs wore clothing that was tight around his buttocks and biceps. The prime points of his physical masculinity were thereby communicated, and not inappropriately, since Communications was what he taught.

While Turner's face was held taut and stiffly attentive, Dobbin's was in constant motion as he acted out his enjoyment of the aria by mouthing words with raised eyebrows, nods, shakes of the head, conducting a phrase one moment and silently singing it the next.

The two of them in their respective attitudes reminded one of the guests, Daniel Hartman, of some imaginary allegory wrought by a sculptor. What was it though? The Wise Man and the Fool? Or The Virgin and the Lecher? Daniel smiled to himself as he watched Turner and Riggs listening. Birgit Nilsson's voice was like a steel blade hacking through a forest of music.

The fourth man, James Donahue, knew little about opera and even less about the other three men.

Francis Turner taught French at the same private college where James, a year earlier, had been hired to teach medieval history. Discreetly surmising that James was discreetly homosexual, Francis had kindly assumed that a small discreet dinner party with two other homosexual men would be welcome to the history scholar. In good taste, of course, the label that bound all of them together would never be mentioned.

The evening was welcomed by James, although he found the air of tomb-like culture surrounding Francis Turner somehow irritating. Dobbin Riggs, with whom James sat on a committee at the college, was merely an ass: friendly enough, but pretentious and dull. The other guest was definitely more interesting. James turned discreetly to look at Daniel and saw that Daniel was likewise observing him. Their eyes met, startled for a moment, and then Daniel camped a rapid imitation of a shrieking opera singer.

James smiled and turned away, his pulse slightly more rapid. So Daniel Hartman was bored too—that was reassuring. Daniel looked intriguingly incongruous in this setting of high culture. His very clothes, loose trousers and a top that resembled a *fin de siècle* painter's smock, played havoc with the controlled and humorless seriousness of Professor Turner's elegant house. Hadn't he been introduced as a librarian?

The aria ended. Francis Turner slowly opened his eyes and rose to remove the record. Dobbin Riggs revived in reverse from his enthusiastic trance, becoming calm and quiet.

"Yes, that was splendid," James said politely.

"What a voice," Daniel said, lighting a cigarette.

"Who was the honey-voiced Huon singing earlier, Francis?" asked Dobbin Riggs, sipping his brandy.

"Señor Domingo." Francis' voice was always quiet and expressionless, indicative of a man lacking even a rudimentary sense of humor.

"I can understand why Rezia would welcome any ship with *him* on board," Dobbin said.

"I think, actually," Francis said musingly, "that I prefer Ingrid Bjoner—"

Daniel broke out with a laugh. "Ingrid Boner?"

"Beeyoner," Francis enunciated. "On the Vanguard Cardinal series, you know. I think I prefer her to Nilsson."

"Yes, and there's a wonderful old Eileen Farrell disc—I think it's deleted now—and she sings it marvelously."

"I heard Grimgerd Windblumen sing Rezia in Copenhagen," Francis reminisced, filling their brandy glassses, "and just where she sees Huon and waves her hanky, Fraulein Windblumen actually leapt into the lake there at Tivoli. My God, her gross tonnage was about the same as the old Queen Mary. I was reminded of Falstaff's, 'I have a kind of alacrity in sinking.'" He allowed no trace of amusement to disfigure his thin, sombre face.

"Then there's that recording of Miss Joan Mushmouth Sutherland singing the aria in English," Dobbin said fussily. "'Ocean, Thou Mighty Monster' it is, although it may as well be in German the way she sings. Not one word is understandable."

"Shocking," Daniel said under his breath.

"I *have* that record," Professor Turner said. "For comparison, why don't I play that, and then the Ingrid Bjoner?"

"Yes, do, that would be interesting," said Dobbin, settling himself into position.

Daniel and James exchanged looks. Already they had heard comparisons of "Io son l'umile ancella" from *Adriana Lecouvreur*, as sung by Leontyne Price, Inge Borkh and Renata Scotto; "When I Am Laid in Earth," from *Dido and Aeneas*, as sung by Price, Janet Baker, Kirsten Flagstad and Victoria de los Angeles; and the "Willow Song" from Verdi's *Otello*, sung by Renata Tebaldi, Gwyneth Jones, Joan Sutherland, Maria Callas, and someone whose voice James and Daniel were barely able to discern above the surface noise of a recording made in 1924.

"Play the Eileen Farrell as well," said Dobbin.

"Yes, I shall," Francis nodded as he flipped through his card catalogue. His record collection was so large that he had been forced to catalogue and cross-reference it in order to find anything. A beautiful old librarian's ladder on wheels was attached to shelves of records that stretched the length and height of one entire wall, so that every rarity was accessible.

"Yes, I shall. Now here's an interesting one—sung by Matthilde Monkgrubber, 1933, but the sound is rather bad."

"Is she the one reputed to have been Hitler's early mistress?" Dobbin asked.

"That's apocryphal, " said Francis.

"Hitler had only one ball," Daniel said. There was a moment of silence. "Did you know that?"

"What is certain," continued Francis, fixing Daniel with a quick disapproving glance, "is that Fraulein Monkgrubber formed a suicide pact with Herr von Wildermann who was—" he continued thumbing through his cards, "—first violin with the Dresden Orchestra and, unfortunately, very married. I was in Germany at the time, at Bayreuth, and—ah, here we are, Farrell/Weber/Oberon." He continued to speak as he mounted the ladder. "And I remember that their bodies were found in a naked putrescent embrace somewhere in Schleswig-Holstein of all places. It was quite a sensation."

"They're always finding bodies in Schleswig-Holstein," Daniel said. "Ritual sacrifices to the fertility goddess used to be made there, and the bodies thrown into the peat, which preserves them. It seems to have been a form of primitive heterosexuality."

"Oh yes, I'd forgotten," said Francis. "I have Gundula Janowitz singing it as well."

"I'm going out on the balcony for some air," Daniel said, rising. "Please go ahead without me."

James, who was attempting to swallow a yawn, quickly rose and said, "If you don't mind, I'll join you." He was instantly aware that Francis and Dobbin were looking at him. He stepped outside after Daniel and slid the glass door closed just as *"Ozean, Du Ungeheuer"* was solemnly beginning to swell once more. Francis and Dobbin had already closed their eyes, like mediums priming themselves for trances.

Professor Turner's home was perched on concrete stilts on one of the highest hills in west Portland. Giant fir trees rose up on either side of his balcony, moving their ponderous branches in the warm February night. A heavy northwest sky pressed down the distant lights of the city. The air was thick with gossip of spring.

The two men stood at the railing, looking down.

"It's beautiful out here, isn't it?" Daniel said. He took a deep breath. "It smells so good."

"I'm afraid they're rather specialized in their musical tastes—too specialized for me," James said.

Daniel let out a soft laugh. "Francis is a brilliant man, but he's so fucking insulated from the world. Isolated. This opera crap. I love opera as much as the next guy, but you have to take it with a hefty grain of salt, you know, or it becomes an obsession."

"Have you known him long?"

"Francis? I took French from him in night school a while back and we slowly got to be friends, despite my despicable pronunciation. Then I helped him catalogue his record collection—it took months. I don't see much of him anymore. I didn't particularly like the circle of closet cases he hangs around with. But he's hidden himself away here for so many years—you know what I mean."

"I'm afraid I don't. This is my first year at the college."

"Oh—well—being a professional person and gay in the teaching profession," Daniel said. "Having to hide who you are for so long eventually has to take its toll, doesn't it?" He folded his arms and looked in through the glass doors at Francis and Dobbin, still in their listening positions.

James cleared his throat. "You don't understand, I think, how difficult it can be for older homosexual men in professions where traditionally there's a great risk involved in being visibly homosexual."

"I do understand," Daniel said. "I understand very well. But I just don't think you should cut yourself off from being, or demanding to be, a part of the world like everyone else, visible if you so choose. And that's what bothers me about Francis and Dobbin and most of their friends. What are they doing with their lives? Their emotional lives. We should all be talking about what it means to be gay, and how things can be changed, instead of listening to the same fucking aria over and over."

"It may not be important for them to talk about it," James said. He was uncomfortable talking about it.

"What's important to hide is important to talk about," Daniel said.

"Did I hear you say you were a librarian?"

"No, you heard Francis say it. Yeah. Special Collections at the University library."

"Enjoy it?"

"Mostly. We have all the old manuscripts and incunabulae and collections of letters—God, the letters people used to write! And then we buy collections and have a lot of good scholars coming in to work with what we have. But when you're a librarian you don't sing, you whisper," Daniel whispered. He moved closer to James on the balcony. "We have a really terrific collection of old herbals. Do you like flowers and herbs and the lore that goes with them?"

"Not particularly, no, except as they relate to my work," James said, his eyes resting longer than he wanted them to on Daniel standing beside him in the fragrant darkness. "As social history they can be important documents."

"As social history *we're* important documents," Daniel said, touching James' arm. "May I see you again?"

James was silent for a moment, excited and uneasy. "If you want to—yes."

"Good. Shall we? One aria down, three more to go." Daniel slid open the glass doors and they went back in just as Francis was playing yet another rendition of *"Ozean, Du Ungeheuer."*

That evening James drove back to the house he and his brother Loren inherited from their parents. Loren had been living in California for some years, and James had only just taken possession of the place, having rented it out to a visiting academic for a year after his father's death.

He was not yet accustomed to smelling the familiar childhood smell of it. The old smells lingered in pockets where he would meet them suddenly, unexpectedly, crossing from one room to another, or opening a door. The smell of his parents, of himself, and Loren, too, he supposed. Ingrained odors of heavy polished furniture, his mother's German cooking, layers of repressive draperies. There were also smells, oddest of all, of partially remembered emotional states—of what happened in certain rooms, certain corners. And an undertow scent of flowers, of roses and lilac, bowls of lavender and spicy pot-pourri. His mother had always had flowers in her house.

James spent his time almost entirely in three rooms: the living room, kitchen, and an upstairs bedroom which had been his as a boy. The rest of the house seemed to live on without him, around him, in a kind of faded, drowsily watchful parental consciousness which at times made him uncomfortable.

Never would James have believed it possible that circumstances would bring him back to live and work in the city, in the very house, where he had been raised. It put him in mind of the goddess Fortuna and her wheel of chance, seen in so much medieval art; Fortuna spinning the absurd destinies of men despite their own desires.

Sometimes in the evening, or on weekends, James would take off a few minutes from his reading or class preparations and slowly wander into the other rooms of the house. Restlessness, he called it. He would stand near the doors, looking in. Rarely would he switch on a light. For what was there to see that he hadn't seen countless times before? The old-fashioned wallpapers with busy floral patterns . . . the rugs, some oriental, others hand-woven rags . . . Meissen figurines and ornamental plates displayed by his mother in glass cabinets . . . an old ticking clock, solemn and mysterious.

It was all here, just as he had known it as a boy, a young man, a returning adult. Never changing. And it seemed at times to be not only dimly watching, but asking for something. At this point in his reveries James would become disgusted with himself and think of selling the place. An anonymous apartment might be better, less weighted with suppressed emotion.

After taking a degree at the university where Daniel was now a librarian, and an M.A. in History at Georgetown, James had spent two years in the army. He was stationed mostly in Germany. From there he went to Yale for his doctorate.

These past ten years of his life, academic and military, were knotted in his brain in such a way that James could never think of them without suppressing a vague prick of panic. Ten years—ten years of his life, and yet never during that decade could James remember feeling that he was living his own life. Whose then was he living?

It was not as if he had floundered along without purpose or direction. On the contrary, his academic career had been direct and certain. He had chosen his field early and his interest had never wavered. But there was something in him that pushed hard, hard; an emotional muscle that never relaxed, never let him be satisfied, that exercised itself but never reached a state of anything more than momentary relief from an inexorable pressure.

When James thought of those ten years, he could only see himself as somehow submerged—doing what he wanted to be doing and yet not being fully alive, as though he were breathing something other than oxygen. When he did surface, as it were, to peer around with print-drenched eyes, and to dry his body in the air shared by a world of fellow-creatures, it was only to experience another kind of puzzling, even hurting, dissatisfaction.

For neither was he at home in that ordinary world where people were simply people, with common emotional and material desires. He longed for contact of some perfect sort, something more than pleasantries or grad student shop-talk. It was that ordinariness that attracted and repelled him, that seemed to expel him even as he looked at it now and again with curious eyes and a hungry heart.

In the army he was forced to appear callous and ordinary. The penalties for being in any way different were severe, if not deadly. And James did appear callous and ordinary. He quickly learned the army's acting requirements. Although he pushed himself, goaded himself, into acquiring the physical stamina and physique required by the army, he had the cushion of an office job during the day. At night, so as not to appear too interested in his language studies and books, he could easily be talked into a night of German beer and *Frauleins*, of loud coarse talk and half-drunken laughter.

There was one soldier with whom he formed a cautious, rather distant attachment. He also became close to a German woman with whom he and his buddy practised their German.

How it happened James never knew. His stomach soured every time he thought of it. The German woman fell in love with him and declared herself. But James had by that time fallen in love with his friend.

He still corresponded with the now Frau Schneider of Munich. But of the soldier to whom he felt himself so passionately attached, the first such person in his life, James had deliberately lost track. He felt lucky to have escaped with his own life and sanity intact.

Until then, aged twenty-four, he hadn't known himself to be particularly sexual, let alone homosexual. Shocked and frightened by this sudden confrontation with an otherwise hidden image of himself, he had gone back with relief to the submerged world of history made hundreds of years earlier. Magna Carta—the Crusades—papal bulls—plagues—Flemish madonnas with serene egg shaped heads—Italian Christs hanging in the full bloody splendor of their crucifixions.

The recognition of something so immediate as his sexuality was like the blinding flash that reveals hidden knowledge or intentions, forever altering inner perspective. Now James' sense of being submerged began to make more sense to him. And he felt that it was imperative to smother "that part" of himself.

What had *this* to do with him? It had happened *to* him without his consent or conscious participation. This was extremely frustrating to the historian who studied causes, reasons.

His work at Yale progressed, though at the cost of his own emotional health. There, in New Haven, on that revered campus, he first heard Fortuna laughing at her spinning wheel of destiny. The submerged but ever-present life grew, despite his will, below full consciousness. What he wanted, and refused at the same time to let himself be, became a vertiginous obsession in its persistent attempts to express itself.

And since he was refusing to acknowledge his homosexuality, James was in another sense admitting to a false guilt. He was telling himself that he was wrong, making himself into an emotional criminal. Criminals can be detected. Their senses hone themselves to razor sharpness. Their lives become dual lives.

It was a nightmare for James. He was ordinary and visible as such, but unseen he was not ordinary at all. His dread was that the invisible part of himself would somehow become known, the finger would be pointed: he would be caught.

Seeing him walking around the campus, sitting in a classroom, arguing with a professor, eating a meal in the cafeteria, who would have guessed the agonies and self-doubts of this upright scholar? Who would have guessed that he still dreamed of a soldier, another man, naked in his arms? Or that he lay awake nights, concocting various potential hells for himself, planning escape routes from Fortuna and her wheel?

No one, for he confided in no one. He drew closer into the very self he refused to be. Vaguely, without knowing why or by whom, he was hoping to be exonerated, forgiven. His savior—the savior of mind and rest—still lived as a presence outside of himself.

Daniel's apartment building was in a state of such architectural decrepitude that prospective tenants were not even asked if they had pets or children.

It was a noisy, door-slamming building, and his apartment had a view of a brick wall from one window and a Catholic church from the other. Paint and scrubbing with disinfectants masked some of the dirt and ancient odors lodged in the very fabric of the place, but the best a too-fussy tenant could do was to accept the building, like death, and live in it until moving elsewhere.

People were always surprised that his two large rooms were as pleasant as they were. The floors were bare and clean, the furniture makeshift but comfortable. Large plants grew in front of the church window, which had a southern exposure, and viney plants needing less light twined on nails around the other.

But why, people wanted to know, why with his decent salary did Daniel not move to a better location? Why did he persist in living (for two years now) in this neighborhood filled with shrieking, dirty children, tipped garbage cans and windows that fluttered the grimy shreds of last winter's plastic insulation?

The easiest answer was that he was paying off his student loans. To answer at all would have been easier if he could honestly say that he loved the area and its inhabitants, that he felt juiced up on humanity's energy when he walked around his neighborhood. For Daniel did love mankind, in a real but increasingly philosophical sort of way. He wanted to see changes made and had been involved in various student protests and radical actions. He would gladly have given up a great deal of personal comfort if it actually meant that needy people would thereby have food in their stomachs and brains.

But when he saw the daily reality, saw how completely engulfed even the poorest of them were by the very aspects of commercial life he considered to be most abhorrent and oppressive, he jumped back a foot or two.

What was it that he saw in his neighborhood? The wrecks of expensive toys, huge cars parked on the ratty streets in a parody of luxury advertising, garbage cans overflowing with junk food wrappers, homes filled with garish overpriced furniture and enormous color televisions that were on day and night.

By now he had no false illusions that his living in the area, the closest thing to a slum that Portland could produce, would in any way balance the cosmic scales. Despite the disillusionment, he continued to try to fit himself in. He had tutored children and teenagers in reading, but they soon lost interest and were too ashamed of their stupidity to accept his patience.

This created a schism between his desire to help and a concomitant certainty that there was no way to help short of giving himself up to it entirely and unquestioningly, all of his life and not just a convenient part of it.

Daniel fairly early on accepted responsibility for his own life, and had, as a consequence, been completely rejected by his parents. He hadn't actually talked to them now for five years, since he was twenty, although an occasional letter arrived from his mother begging him to give up a life of depravity and offering him the assistance and assurance of her prayers.

He had not been forced to tell them that he was gay. He had deliberately chosen to do so, exercising the free will he had always been taught was man's salvation. But in their furious quest for a comforting, impossible perfection, Daniel's parents controlled all emotional situations by instantly deciding their sin-content and then acting quickly and accordingly on God's behalf.

They decided that he was doing this because he wanted to sin, because he was weak, confused, because, because, because . . . none of their bizarre explanations even vaguely approaching the calm stubborn reality of the situation. Mr. and Mrs. Hartman refused to countenance individual psychology. Everything could be cured by prayer. And their son was perverse, damned, so long as he insisted on following behavior so antithetical to Christian belief.

Of course Daniel hadn't stepped into or provoked these nerve-rattling scenes without some premonition of what would happen. They unfolded around him with a sharp, terrible expectedness. Always there was the hope that their natural parental love could in some way be fitted into the pitiless demands of God's law. But that hope turned sour as he saw clearly and for the first time how their love was based on exclusion instead of inclusion.

When they heard the voice of God telling them to obtain their son's repentance or to renounce him forever—like Abrahams commanded to butcher their offspring—they raised their knives to the task. Only, unfortunately, there was no thick feathery rustle of wings, no touch from the ecstatic finger of an angel, no last minute stay of emotional execution.

Why had he done it? It had changed his vision. Suddenly he saw the staggering cruelty and stupidity that dominated even the most well-meaning people. Perhaps particularly those. He had to cast far and wide for ways to assimilate the knowledge of this particularly intimate hostility without letting it destroy him. He sought ways to reject it and accept himself.

It was at this time in his life that he met Tilda, one of those kindred spirits who make life worth living despite disappointments, dilemmas and disillusionment. Tilda took him into her heart in a way he had never been taken before. From her he learned to trust love again. The way she lavished her emotions appealed to a part of Daniel that had always been crimped. Their hearts grew deeper as they nursed one another through every ensuing crisis in their lives.

James had a date and he was simultaneously so excited that he was unable to concentrate on his reading, and so nervous that his stomach churned with bilge. He forced himself to sit in his straight-backed reading chair, but his eyes followed the print only out of habit and saw nothing. At a quarter to eight he allotted himself fifteen minutes to get dressed. He had deliberately to retard all of his movements, though this did not calm him down and in fact increased his excitement. A few times he sneezed, another indication of emotional agitation.

Slowly he undressed, looking briefly at his body in the mirror. He sniffed under his armpits to be certain that they smelled like the pine forest advertised on the deodorant label. He was thirty-six years old and thought of his body as on its last legs. Yes, it was still trim, but how long would *that* last?

He had never thought of himself as particularly attractive, though this was more out of spite towards himself than based on his image in a mirror. He was tall and fair-skinned, with black barbered hair and walnut brown eyes, a prominent nose he was secretly proud of and lips that were habitually compressed into a slightly crooked, slightly disapproving line. Recently hair had started to sprout from his ears and diminish on his scalp, certain signs of impending decrepitude.

James was the sort of teacher on whom students were forever developing crushes. They saw him as well-dressed, severe, scholarly, mysterious, meticulous, and unmarried, attributes perennially welcome in the fantasy love life of college students. Anonymous typed love poems ("You have impregnated your soul in mine/I carry you gently, lest we miscarry") had been slipped under his door and into his mailbox, and in classes he often caught eyes that were dreaming not of the vicious Crusades, not of the fall of Constantinople or the Great Schism, but of him, certainly.

All the more reason to be wary and especially nervous tonight. If he and Daniel went out somewhere, there was the possibility, even the likelihood, that someone would see them together. Inferences would be drawn . . . heads bow together and lips begin to move . . .

He brushed his hair again—it had been slightly mussed while he was dressing—and took another look at himself, twitching his shoulders to get his shirt to fit perfectly. Yes, all right. He slipped on his glasses, tortoise-shell and of a kind seemingly invented for professors, and left the house.

At first he was convinced that Daniel had given him the wrong address. In the glare of a streetlamp he read the numbers he had written down. A sharp east wind set the few trees down the street in motion and gave the night a mind of its own. James entered the building and found the apartment.

But surely it was the wrong apartment. He heard voices—plural, more than one—someone else was there. Immediately apprehensive, James began to sweat through his antiperspirant.

He had assumed that Daniel would be alone and now wondered if he should leave, for what would this other person, or persons, think when he entered? Would Daniel have told them that . . . ?

His guilty, racing thoughts were here interrupted by singing. Two voices, one male, one female, were singing some soft song. James stood listening outside the door until footsteps came clattering down a nearby stairwell. He quickly turned so that his face would not be seen and rapped at the door.

Immediately, from within, there was silence, then hushed voices again, footsteps approaching the door, the door opening, the door open.

It was a woman wearing high heels and a towel. Her frizzy blonde hair was pulled up into a quivering knot on top of her head. Damp strands of loose hair floated around her neck. "Hello, darling, you're James and I'm Tilda," she said. "Come in. Pleased to meet you."

"Is Daniel here?" James asked.

"He's in the tub. Someone was sick at the library and he had to stay late. We biked here as fast as we could and then I insisted that we take a hot bath to relax."

"Hello, hello," came Daniel's voice from the bathroom. "James? Sorry I'm not ready."

"You're not sorry at all," Tilda called back. "You deserve a hot bubble bath and what does half an hour matter in the scheme of things anyway?" She said in a low, confidential voice to James: "He's been working very hard lately, cataloguing some weird old material that has all sorts of funny clauses attached to it."

"Tild, will you please pour James something to drink?"

"But of course, my lamb. We're imbibing a cheap dry Cabernet Sauvignon from the Sonoma valley, all right?" James nodded. Tilda handed him a glass and said in a professional hostess voice, "Let's go into the bathroom, shall we? It's nice and cozy in there. That's Sylvie craving a pat like the rest of us." A large smiling retriever suddenly appeared, frantically waving a plumy tail.

"Sit, darling!" Tilda commanded. The dog, with a groan of pleasure, sat. "Now shake! Show James your pretty nails." Up came a paw with pink nails. James shook it.

He followed Tilda, naked except for her towel and high heels, feeling as though he had dived into a fast dream that he was powerless to control. The bathroom was small and steamy, very aromatic. Its walls had been painted to look like an ancient frescoed Roman villa.

"It's based on Livia's Garden in Rome," Tilda said, seeing James' astonished face. "My husband Brenner did it."

Several lit candles on shelves of varying height threw strange flickering patterns onto the walls, picking out tawny fruits and flying birds among the blue-green coloration.

Submerged in the tub with faintly crackling bubbles dissolving around him was Daniel, his face damp, his hair wet around the neck and ears. When James and Tilda entered he raised himself so that his broad shoulders were exposed.

James found all of this terribly erotic.

Tilda pointed to a small stool at the end of the tub and James, with his wine, nervously perched himself on it. Tilda sat on the toilet seat and lit a cigarette.

"Tilda is the sort of friend a person finds once in a lifetime," Daniel said, reaching up with a dripping hand to pat hers. "The sort of person you can be naked with."

James had for a moment been lulled by the room and its warmth into feeling slightly relaxed. Well, almost. But now, suddenly, he was again distancing himself from accepting the situation at hand by a vague sense of danger, of being found out. He imagined Tilda whispering to someone, "Do you know Professor Donahue? He came over to see Daniel and we sat in the bathroom and watched Daniel take a bath." The story would change, transmute, until he was in the bath with Daniel, or all three of them together.

He cleared his throat and said, "I heard you singing."

"A talent scout!" Tilda said. She jumped up and did a quick tap routine in her high heels. "Actually, it was a little French madrigal Daniel found in one of the books he's cataloguing." She closed her eyes and shyly began to sing the song again. Her voice was high and sweet. Daniel joined in with his baritone.

"Very nice," James said. "All I understood was *'petite fleur.'*"

"That's all you need to understand," Daniel said. "It's about the life of one. This little flower. It rises from the dark singing earth and opens its eyes to the sun."

"It watches and grows until its life is done," Tilda added.

"Plucked," Daniel said, "although your rhyme is better. You're looking handsome tonight, James."

"I am?"

"I love that sweater," Tilda said, feeling the wool on James' arm. "And on that tactile note, my dears, I must bid you *adieu.*" She leaned over the tub and kissed Daniel. "Call me tomorrow. If Brenner's going to spend all day in his studio again, maybe we can meet for coffee downtown."

"I want to see your new painting."

"Not until I'm satisfied and finished with it. If I ever am."

"You're too hard on yourself. You're keeping yourself from finishing it, if you want my dime-store theory."

"Probably I am," Tilda sighed, discarding her towel in front of James' astonished eyes. She stood, naked except for high heels, looking down at Daniel in the tub. "I'm scared of Brenner's eye on it," she said as she began to pull on her clothes.

"It's your work," Daniel said, "not Brenner's."

"I know, I know."

"I'll give you a massage tomorrow if you want one."

"Have I ever said no to the pressure of hands on my body? Bye sweetie. Nice meeting you, James."

"I'd see you out but my bubbles are wilting," Daniel said.

When she had gone, James felt his eyes unaccountably drawn to everything in the room except Daniel, lying in the tub.

"I'm glad you came," Daniel said, sitting up. The hair on his chest was thicker than James had imagined, and this slow exposure of his wet, naked body, a piece at a time, James found as erotic and nerve-wracking a vision as anything he had ever seen. The situation was crazily normal and friendly, but dangerously seductive at the same time. The steamy heat, the garden-painted walls, so stylized and tender, the candles and the light they threw, the deep earth-like fragrance of whatever was in the bathwater, even the small amount of wine he had drunk, made this room a place which existed in no senses that he previously possessed. Bacchus might enter next. He smiled when Daniel spoke but could think of nothing to say in return.

"I'm about to rise from the water, and you're welcome to stay," Daniel said. "I don't want to embarrass you, though, if you think you'd be embarrassed."

"Embarrassed?"

"Tilda and I have gotten into the habit of heart-to-hearts in the tub. But I should have thought of you—that you might not be comfortable."

"Shall I leave then?"

Daniel laughed and rose dripping, his skin flushed.

"Some way to begin a first date, eh?"

James, pretending to sip casually the rest of his wine, sitting on a low stool in front of a naked young man, had to agree that indeed it was.

After four or five dates they still had not slept together. Certain looks had been exchanged, but James refused to make the first move and Daniel was made shy, or perhaps apprehensive, by James' careful distancing. Of course the prospect became all the more exciting the longer they delayed.

James had never been able to instigate a sexual encounter—or, indeed, any encounter that was not absolutely necessary or formally expected. He would never have been the one to ask Daniel out. Colleagues were asked to his home only after he had gone to theirs, and then it was once only, and only because etiquette demanded reciprocity.

James had set up an exacting system of weights and balances in his life. Sexually, perhaps, this was understandable. If he did not make the first move, he was less guilty. He was responding to rather than seeking after. Over the years he had vaguely tricked himself into believing that he was less homosexual if the first move was never his. His sex life seemed to exist in a court of law, with his own passivity as his only defense.

And yet he often hoped, he hoped now with Daniel, that the move would be made soon. He wanted it to happen.

He would not, however, actively place himself in a situation where he could be rejected. From the beginning, from his first attachment to his friend in the army, James had only felt terror at the idea of making his love and longings known.

Everything, to James, now depended on Daniel.

In some ways, Daniel was for him a dangerous person: an emotional person. But, like the hungry beggar seeing food on the rich man's table, James looked on with excitement and a furtive delight. Emotions were not something James recognized.

In James' version, most homosexuals were unstable people waiting for breakdowns and periodically attempting suicide. So it was with relief that he saw Daniel not fitting into the grotesque parody of gay life concocted from his own fears. Daniel's naturalness was what attracted and intrigued him.

But what was all of this leading to? He was on a path he didn't know and there were no bread crumbs for him to follow. Where would a sexual and emotional attraction end? James adamantly refused to believe in the possibility that he could be happy with "that part" of his life.

After dinner and a particularly bad movie, they entered Daniel's apartment and heard Sylvie's nails clicking on the bare floor as she came over, heavy with sleep, to greet them. Daniel crouched down in the darkened room, scratching and whispering doggie endearments to which Sylvie responded with a drawn-out groan of pleasure.

James stood behind, as he always did, the guest who must wait for an invitation to be seated. He had always been uneasy around affectionate animals. As a child he had never been allowed pets, and he found it impossible to reduce his consciousness to a level that an animal could understand and share.

As he looked down at Daniel, his eyes adjusting to the darkness and clarifying Daniel's figure, he suddenly had to fight back a fantasy that mounted to a roar and almost demanded an impulsive action.

He saw himself first putting his hands on Daniel's thick, rough-looking hair, smoothing, stroking it. And then when Daniel turned around (as he did in the fantasy), James put his fingers on Daniel's face. He felt Daniel's skin, his high cheekbones, his nose, ears, mouth . . . and when Daniel gave him his strong, broad hands, James pulled him up, drew that tall body close. The body he had already seen naked and had once dreamed of, though he refused to remember the dream, all dreams. James stood trembling, although twitching might be a better word, hoping that this scene would materialize, that someone other than James would take command of his body and force him to move, to begin. He could think of nothing he wanted more.

And then, suddenly, Daniel did stand, and turned to face him. They said nothing. The silence accumulated itself, mixed with the darkened room to create a place removed from James' ordinary perceptions. What am I doing here? he frantically asked himself. What is going to happen? What am I going to do?

A blind energy seeking release through the expression of his desire ran through James. But there also came a sudden souring vision of a watching waiting classroom, all eyes turned upon him to infect and guiltify the fantasy. He saw Daniel standing there, looking at him, and felt a weight in his body, as though his blood had thickened, ossified, turned him to stone.

"Well?" Daniel said.

"I enjoyed the evening," James said, by this time barely able to speak. "Very much. Except for the film." He could see Daniel's white teeth as he laughed. "What do you find so amusing?" he asked, his voice hurt.

"I'm not laughing because I'm amused, but because I'm nervous."

"Why should you be nervous?"

"Romance makes me nervous."

"Romance?" James quickly tossed the word back.

"Nasty word, isn't it."

"It's one I don't think we—I—should use."

"Should we sit and discuss semantics?" Daniel said. "The semantics of romantics?"

"No."

"Then what should we do?"

"I don't know," said James.

"For Christ's sake, it's absurd to stand here in the dark whispering like this. And to feel nervous."

"Is it I who makes you nervous?"

"Of course it's you. I don't normally come home and stand in the dark and feel nervous."

"I don't want you to feel nervous."

"You have that effect on me. Just now anyway."

"Why?"

"Because I sense what you want and your fear—your reluctance—to make any sort of move to let me know you want it."

"What is it I want?"

"Me," Daniel said simply.

"You're a very attractive young man." Again Daniel's teeth shone as he laughed. "Attractive in ways that aren't just physical," James said.

"Are you afraid of me?" Daniel asked.

"I can't—I can't come any closer than with words."

Daniel was silent for a moment. "You mean you're impotent?"

"No—no . . . well, yes, in some ways I suppose I am." James started when Daniel took his hand. He had to break the reflex that immediately wanted him to step back, away, from the very contact he desired.

"If you need kid gloves, I'll give you kid gloves," Daniel said, and led him into the next room. There was a low simple bed, and he gently pushed James down onto it. "Relax for Christ's sake," he whispered, and kissed him. "Relax your lips—they feel like they've been starched."

"Too many boring lectures have passed through them," James said nervously.

"This has nothing to do with lectures—just the way you feel about yourself."

"Not much, I'm afraid."

"But, you see, what you fail to realize is how I feel about you." Again Daniel kissed him.

James lay quietly, tensely, as Daniel unbuttoned his shirt, pulled it free from his trousers and arms and ran his hand over James' bare chest. He pulled off James' shoes and stockings, undid his belt, unzipped his pants and removed them.

"Sexy undies," Daniel said.

James closed his eyes as his underwear was slipped down his legs. There he lay, naked and exposed, on Daniel's bed.

"I'm afraid I'm not circumsized," he whispered.

"Lucky you," Daniel said, taking James' already hard cock in his hand. Smiling, he lay down beside James. "You're really beautiful," he said.

"Please don't say such absurd things," James said. "I'm perfectly aware that my body is not particularly attractive."

Daniel let out a breath of exasperation. "I don't say things that I don't mean. So accept what I say as being true to me."

"I had polio as a child. I had to work very hard to make my body look halfway decent. Especially my legs. Every day I had to show myself. It was humiliating and very painful."

"You don't have polio now," Daniel said.

"No, but in some ways you always have it. Like Catholicism."

Daniel said nothing.

"Are you going to lie there and observe me? I feel as if I'm in a zoo."

"Want to undress me?"

"No," James whispered, beside himself with excitement. "Not this time. I want to watch you."

Daniel got up and opened the window shade. He stood for a moment looking out. The budding branches of a tree threw pale shadows across him and into the room. "Beautiful night," he said. "The moon's almost full, and the church looks almost friendly." He pulled off his clothes. He stood naked. He crossed the room and lay down beside James.

The fantasy had materialized. It was taking place. A crazy sense of gratitude lifted James' heart. He was so excited that he forgot several times to keep his eyes closed to the proceedings. In his excitement he forgot, too, what a bad lover he assumed himself to be.

Daniel's body was beside his, beneath his, on top of his . . . his lips were on James' lips, on James' flesh. Daniel's tongue roused virgin parts of him that he had never known could be roused. His body had been that of a dignified sleeping prince, so long dulled that it had nothing left to dream and no reason to wake. But now he feared this awakening as much as he revelled in the new consciousness it presented.

The experience, unlike his few clumsy others, was neither empty nor an end in itself. He could not feel the shame that he thought he should feel. A sense of shared physical elation in an act of love buoyed him up and carried him on . . . until Sylvie, bored with her corner, clicked into the room and settled herself with a sigh, head on paws, facing them.

At that moment James' outer consciousness, the one constructed of shocked faces, law courts, spying eyes, fingers pointed to pages in the Bible, dismissal and humiliation, engulfed him in a stinking wave. His body changed, tensed, became clumsy, uncertain. He wanted to roll onto his side and close his eyes.

"What's wrong?" Daniel asked. "Is something wrong?"

"I'm sorry . . . I'm sorry."

"Don't be sorry, just tell me what's wrong."

"It's idiotic . . . the dog."

Daniel was puzzled. "Sylvie is idiotic?"

"No, no—I mean the dog here, in the room. I'm sorry. I feel ridiculous. It bothers me."

Daniel sat up, snapped his fingers, and told Sylvie to leave. With a few tentative wags of her tail she did so, but they heard her muttering as she resettled herself in the next room.

"Is that better?" Daniel asked.

"You must think I'm insane!"

Daniel laughed. "So we all have weird little things that bother us. She's gone now."

"I feel like an absolute fool!" James groaned.

"Don't feel like a fool." Daniel hung over James' face, amused and aroused. "Feel the way you were feeling, like a bonafide lover."

"I don't know if I can."

"Let's start again, where we left off. Do you want to?"

James pulled him close. "Yes, yes, I do."

"Getting serious, isn't it," Tilda said. Daniel was sitting in her small studio, which was the front room of the tiny house she and her husband Brenner rented. Large windows looked out onto the windy, cloud-crazy Oregon day. Fits of rain periodically drenched the street and sidewalk, followed by a hot wet sheen of sun. "How long have you been seeing old James now?"

"Since February—four and a half months."

"Are you in love with him?"

"Yes."

"I mean, darling, in *love* with him. The real thing."

"The real thing."

"Sweetie, love is supposed to make you happy—you know, tra-la-la and all tingly and effervescent. Sort of like an Alka Seltzer in gin."

"I know. Sometimes I do feel like that. Most of the time I do. There is some sort of life, something you do feel without trying to force it. Something extra."

"Why so blue then? I mean why beside the fact that it's been raining every fucking day for the past three months and everyone in Portland is depressed to the point of insanity?"

Daniel sniffed the branches of apple blossom she was drawing. The room was saturated with their clean, soapy fragrance. "I don't think he loves me. If he did, I don't think he could say so."

Tilda set her tea cup down with a crack. "Jesus fucking H. Christ."

"What?"

"The way our lives seem to mirror one another's. Isn't this just what I've rattled on about to you a hundred million times about Brenner?"

"I suppose it is. I just don't understand this fear of emotion. Yes, I do too understand it. I understand it perfectly well."

"Most men hate emotion," Tilda said. "It makes them feel out of control."

"I think with James it's a fear of being gay. Or not of being gay itself, but of being caught being gay. Being found out."

"You know sometimes I wish Brenner was gay, and that was why we had these problems. I could at least have something tangible to understand then."

"How do you know he isn't?" Daniel said, smiling at her.

"Darling, just because a man likes a finger jammed up his asshole when he's fucking you doesn't mean that he's gay. Every man I've ever fucked has liked that, and believe me, none of them were gay."

They laughed.

"You know what it is?" Daniel said. "It's a fear of being thought of as feminine. Don't you think? Women are supposed to be emotional, and men are supposed to be strong and stern. Unequivocable."

"I know—it's such utter bullshit."

"And being emotional must be thought of as distracting somehow. Debilitating. A kind of hindrance to getting ahead, whatever that is."

"A nuisance, yes."

"But Christ, how can people let themselves live without it? Without allowing themselves the pleasure of feeling?"

"Because, old pal, there's also the pain of feeling."

"Don't I know."

Tilda moved over to where he sat and pulled his head to her breasts. "Dan, I love you because you're not that way. Not afraid of yourself. Even from the first day we met you weren't like that."

"Ten years ago."

"God, just think of us then—talking about Love and Art and planning our Futures."

"And just think all we've learned in the meantime: that we can't plan our Futures as easily as all that because Love can't be Love . . . "

"And the Art World is nasty and vicious."

"And Emotions are dangerous."

"And marriage." Tilda rose with a sputter. "Ha! Marriage can be as ghastly and awful as our parents' marriages. Oh dear," she said, her eyes sparkling with laughter, "all we've gone through together. And will go through together, pals to the end. Just think when we're eighty and hobbling about in our rest home. Just think of all that will be behind us then. We'll think we've lived these perfectly fascinating lives, and all of our children and grandchildren—"

"Your children and grandchildren."

"Yes, but who knows," she said with an easy wave of her hand, "someday maybe you'll have some too. They'll all sit around as bored as skunks while we rattle on and on about all we've seen and done and experienced back in the Olden Days. Before 2000 A.D. And then they'll leave and say to one another, 'Jeez, what a couple of old bores those two are.'"

"Maybe they'll be curious and ask what things were like back in 1971."

"Eighty years old," Tilda said. "Really, it seems like so little."

"I'll be dead long before that, my dear."

"How do you know?" Tilda asked quickly.

Daniel shrugged. "Just something I know."

"Don't be so fucking ridiculous! And don't you dare tell me what age you think you'll be when you die because I don't want to know. Who knows what will have happened to death by then?" She looked out of the window, chewing on the inside of her mouth, as a thin monotonous rain began to fall. "Of course I only want to live as long as I have all my faculties. As far as I'm concerned there's nothing wrong with quietly putting yourself away when you start losing big chunks of what made you you. I'm not going to end up like my Granny, senile and bedridden and with no bowel or bladder control, just a sad little puzzlement to herself. That's a parody of life."

"Tildy, my dear, you'll never be a parody of life. I'll pull the plug on the respirator for you, if you want me to."

"But I'd see your big blue eyes and your skinny intense face that last second and shriek, 'Hold it! There's something I haven't told you yet!' I'd be afraid of missing something, and it would be so boring and lonely to die and not be able to discuss it with you over tea." She went back to her easel. "I don't want to talk about it anymore. What are you going to do about James?"

"See what happens, I guess, whatever that means."

"It means that you want him to be in love with you. That's simple enough."

"Yes, but I refuse to force him."

"My dear, the man *needs* forcing. Like a bulb in winter. Like a dish full of narcissus bulbs."

"And what then? What comes after he says, if he ever does, that he loveth me?"

"Darling, then you say, 'And I, James, loveth you.'"

"It all sounds too ridiculous. Why do we have to be so self-conscious about love? It's such a simple thing—"

"Simple it's not. It should be, yes, but it's not. It's huge and complicated and full of fear and insecurity and bogeymen."

"But it's the most important thing," Daniel said.

"When the time comes, you'll know what to do and do it."

"Love," Daniel sniffed. He sighed and looked into his cup as though the tea leaves there might have some explanation for it. "You know, it really is a changer of things."

"I know," said Tilda.

"Things get shifted around in you and held up to the light."

Tilda daubed his nose with a wet paintbrush. "Did you learn that when you were with Jacob?"

"Yes. And from you."

In the way that certain things in shared lives are appropriated without being granted or asked for, the gardens were Daniel's from the first moment he saw them.

There was still no mention of living together, no vows or declarations of love, but in some quiet intangible way James and Daniel were approaching an acknowledgement that their relationship was something more than tentative and temporary.

This was a terrifying idea for James, an impossibility that should remain an impossibility and not mutate into reality. Endless problems, endless complications would come of it, and of course it would end, turn flat and sour, he was certain of that. He would lose his precious solitude, his very freedom.

Yet here he was, on a Saturday morning in July, showing

Daniel his house for the first time. It was obvious to both of them that this was a symbolic gesture, for James had been adamant until now about not bringing Daniel ("that part" of him) home.

The house was separate from any acknowledgement of James' sexual or emotional life. It was detached from any life at all. Around it birds wove a shifting, piercing, lively net of sound; the note-jammed air was palpable with their speech. Possums trundled and rustled about in the dark. A fox lived in a nearby meadow and could sometimes be heard barking at night. One morning James had been surprised to see a deer nibbling near the back terrace doors. Pairs of swans regally glided past on the cold, fresh waters of the river. The luxuriousness of the plant life spoke with leaves and flowers of the eternal currents of growth in the soil. But within all this the house sat like a brain stubbornly sleeping through a life of change, refusing to do anything more than guard its own quiet misery.

There was a spell on the house. Daniel could feel it, though he said nothing. And what was more amazing to him was that James accepted it. Daniel could see James' nervousness, could see how James was reverential and resentful of any too-obvious intrusion of life upon its slumbers. Was the place asleep or dead?

Daniel was quietly whisked through the halls, quickly shown each room, and led on. It was a tour of a museum in which the objects had taken over and become resentful of eyes upon them. In one spacious, high-ceilinged bedroom, Daniel pulled back the heavy draperies from the windows. Light rushed in, settling itself like a loud buzzing audience in a theater, picking out details and objects that had forgotten they were meant to be seen.

The effect was so startling, the change so immediate, that he flung out a hand to exclaim over it and knocked a small china figurine from the dresser beside him. Before he realized what happened, James had rushed over, quickly examined the figurine, and set it back in its place.

"I'm sorry! Is it broken?"

"Slightly chipped, that's all."

Daniel carefully picked it up to look. "Oh God, her nose has come off. She looks in the last stages of syphilis now, thanks to me. I suppose it's some rare German piece worth thousands of dollars?"

"No." James clenched his hands in his pockets, watching carefully as Daniel replaced the figurine on the dresser. "It's something I gave to my mother for Christmas one year. She collected such things as you see."

"This was their bedroom?"

"Yes."

"It's nice—in a crowded way. You know what's wonderful? The view from these windows. I can't imagine the pleasure of waking up and having my eyes start the day with such calm beauty. Come—look." He held out his hand but James only pressed it. They stood together for a moment looking out into the gardens behind the house, and then James moved away.

Daniel pulled up a recalcitrant window and a sweet billow of air rushed in to enliven the stale room. He crouched beside the open window, looking out. "Unfair, unfair, unfair."

"What is?"

"All this," Daniel said, nodding out the window. "Not being seen. Why don't you sleep in here for Christ's sake?"

"No—I wouldn't want to."

"Is the room you're in now the room you had as a boy? The one facing the street with the wisteria outside it?"

"Yes. It's been changed since then of course."

Daniel turned back into the flow of air from the window. "I can't get over it. All this behind one curtain. Looking out on it gives me the strangest feeling." The moment he said this he knew what the feeling was. Something was being revealed to him, on trust. Down in the gardens, he saw an old woman. She slowly walked into view from a dark, overgrown path, a basket of cut roses on her arm, stood in the center of the garden and lifted her head. She looked at Daniel. The hairs rose on his neck and arms. She walked away, disappearing down another path.

James, unaware of all of this, did not ask Daniel what the "strange feeling" was. He saw Daniel rise very suddenly, his face altered, and rub his arms. James closed the window and they left the room. He returned later that evening, alone, to look once again at the figurine and to pull the draperies.

When they stood at the terrace doors, Daniel again felt unaccountably apprehensive and excited. He put his hand on James' back as the doors were unlocked and opened. Sylvie, who had been sequestered during the tour, tore out and scattered a group of sparrows and robins. James and Daniel, squinting, stepped out onto the fan-shaped brick courtyard.

"And this," James said, "is the back yard. What you saw from upstairs."

"No, don't call it a yard. Not a yard. That's too unmagical. A garden. Call it your garden." Daniel's eyes moved back and forth as if reading what he saw, moving up to the blanket of clear summer sky, down to the gravel and grass paths visible between overgrown hedges. Sight then was vision, a new seeing, a reseeing, a sudden meaning. His heart had begun to beat very fast in a kind of expanding suspense and surprise.

"It used to be a garden, at any rate," James said, stubbing with the toe of his shoe a clump of plantain growing between the brick. "My mother planned them—they were hers. When she died, my father let them go."

Don't say anything, thought Daniel. He knew he had been entrusted with a vision. It had happened before. "Grief?" he said. "Is that why your father let them go?"

"Old age, mostly."

"Or indifference. He could have hired a gardener. You could have helped. You've let them go too."

"I wasn't here then. After college and the army I was teaching in Washington until I came back here. When could I have done anything?" he said in the voice of the accused. "Anyway, I'm not a gardener. Too much work." He kicked at another clump of plantain, looking uneasily out into his mother's gardens, now wildly overgrown and asserting their freedom. "My father never felt much for them, I think. Them or it, what is it when you're talking about gardens?"

"Both," Daniel said. Suddenly he laughed. "Yeah, both. Singular in the sense of extraordinary, and cohesiveness. But plural in the sense of variety." An unaccountable flame of delight leapt through his body. His eyes danced about, swept through the colors. The greens were so dense against the sky that they clung to his eyeballs. It had rained in the night and the sun licked with a gentle tongue the puddles in the paths, drawing up the summer breath of the gardens. There was absolute silence . . . and no silence at all, for the resounding birdsong was fierce with joy. "Man, I don't understand how someone—anyone—couldn't *feel* for this! It's so beautiful!"

"Well he did help," James said. "He fussed around clipping and cutting grass. But I don't think he ever really thought much about them. It was just a yard to him, pleasant in its own way. He never knew anything about flowers."

"I don't want to hear about your father's *not* doing anything out here. I want to hear about your mother, the one who did. She was the active one out here, the positive one."

"My father was active," James said quickly.

"Yes, but not in the way she was, out here. She loved roses, didn't she?"

"She used to come out here early in the morning with a basket and fill it with roses," James said.

Daniel pointed down the center path towards the river. "Can't you see how this was planned? Just the perspective here. Carefully planned, and meant to be cared for."

"My mother studied and worked in a botanical garden in Germany before she came to America."

"This is getting better and better," Daniel said. "Did she teach botany or landscaping here? Did she design other gardens, or what?"

"No," James said, "she married my father and gave it all up."

"She never gave it up," Daniel said. "It's all right here. Her secret sense of—"

"Sense of what?"

Daniel shrugged and sat down on a low stone wall marking off the terrace. "Sense of everything. Of life. Of the design of life."

James looked at Daniel, at the person eleven years younger than himself, the one so much freer. Daniel, who slept with him on a small bed in a two-room apartment: a person still new in his life, still surprising in his un-go-awayable reality.

Daniel, who was all the while staring out into the waiting gardens. Already they were haunting him, drawing him in. He slowly stepped down, seeming to know without seeing them, feeling them comfortable to his feet, the three wide bluestone steps that descended to what had evidently been a kitchen garden, full of perennial herbs. He had a sense that he was wading out into something that had been waiting for him.

Sylvie came bounding up to him with a stick in her mouth which he obligingly threw for her to fetch. James followed a step or two behind, watching him.

"So as a boy," Daniel said, "you ran up and down these paths and always had this . . . sense of beauty and mystery around you."

"First of all, it didn't always look like this," James said. "Before my mother's work on it, this was all grass and a few trees. The work was gradual. And second of all, when I had polio I didn't do any running anywhere for a very long time."

"A grassy field," Daniel said. "She knew somehow the way things would look years later. Such patient eyes she must have had. Your mother was a real artist, you know that?" He held out his hand. "Let's explore some of these paths."

James took Daniel's hand, but self-consciously, as if he might turn around and see someone—mother or father or colleague or neighbor—standing in the French doors, watching. Eyes, eyes, eyes: eyes in the trees, behind leaves, in the ferns, behind the bamboo. There was no way anyone could see into the garden, James was perfectly aware of this, but long careful acceptance of the watching, waiting eyes, eyes ready to pounce and denounce, made him uneasy.

"Man, you are lucky to have this!" Daniel said as they walked down the path. "A curse on you for neglecting it, though."

"I would have thought you'd rather see it natural and doing what it wants to do, rather than being disciplined by the hand of man."

"No, not here. You can't just leave it and have it remain as beautiful as it's meant to be. Don't you get it? This is a piece of art. There are certain effects your mother wanted to achieve here, colors and forms and some overall plan. And all that requires care. Haven't you ever seen this?" Daniel asked in his amazement.

"I suppose I haven't. I see a lot of different things, if that's what you mean."

"When it goes to seed, and gets completely out of control, it spoils what she was after."

"And how do you know what she was after?" James said tersely.

"I can feel it," Daniel said simply. "And see it here as we walk."

"I have too many things to do," James said, his voice tightening in his throat. "That house to keep in some semblance of order, not to mention class preparations and committee reports and—"

"It's a big place for one person," Daniel said.

"Sometimes I think it would be better to rent it out again, or to sell it, if my brother would agree."

"Sell it?" Daniel's voice turned sharp. "And just leave it? Leave this? Don't you see what's here? Don't you feel it?"

"I've told you: I do somewhat," James said coolly. It was true that he was not seeing what Daniel was seeing. He did not connect his mother's gardens with emotions except of a faint, anonymous, vaguely pleasurable kind.

"I do feel something here," Daniel said. "I know you distrust that word because it doesn't mean anything tangible to you. But I have to say that I do. To have a garden like this, a place where lovers and gentle souls could walk; a place of quiet and complete acceptance. A sort of mirror of what you feel, or want to feel. It would be wonderful."

"And a great deal of very hard work," James said.

"Work's unpleasant only when you don't feel connected to it. *I* could do the work," Daniel said.

If it had been any other place, any other time, Daniel's mind might not have taken hold of these gardens, the idea of them, the possibilities he saw contained within them. But his vision had been immediate and was already drawing things together. He was full of the energy an artist feels when his next work descends upon him, and he could not suppress the urgency he felt. "Let me come here and change your unseeing," he said.

James was not a person to be easily persuaded by excited suggestions or enthusiasms. He froze when Daniel said this because he was not willing to think of anyone other than himself, alone, living in the house. But now Daniel had suggested it, and a terrible pressure was instantly pumping through James' veins a tension he did not know how to release. Daniel was making him want what he would not let himself have. "Don't," he said, turning away. "It's so easy to be dramatic on the spur of the moment. I don't want dramatics."

"No, you don't want anything. Or rather you do, but you refuse to give any of it to yourself. What the hell are you fighting?"

"You," James said.

"For me or against me?"

"Both—both."

"Yes, but—look, you force what you call dramatics because you don't let things move naturally along the way. You stall everything. How much longer do you think I can be quietly patient? You stop me. You take what you want from me and then run back here to be alone and pretend that I'm not real."

"I don't pretend that. You are real. Too real. If you want to force me to say such things, there, you can be satisfied."

"You're saying them yourself, James. I'm not forcing you."

"I told you once, a long time ago, that I was an impossible person, and that you couldn't expect things from me. I can't give them."

"You think you can't. You think you won't. But you do, in ways you don't even know."

"Why do you bother with me?" James asked. "That's what I don't understand. Why do you continue to see me and—sleep with me. There must be younger men you'd be more compatible or comfortable with."

Daniel growled with frustration. "Don't you see that it's *you* that I find endearing?"

"If you find me so endearing why aren't you willing to let me be who I am?" James countered.

"I am willing, and I do let you be who you are—your real personality. What I'm fighting is the one you've superimposed on top of it. The tragic one. The one that accepts guilt and misery. That's not you, James. It doesn't have to be."

The truth punched James hard. This was not a revelation

to him. He knew he was stalling himself with Daniel, with his own emotions, because without Daniel he could still feel that he exerted some control over his life, over "that part" of himself. He was afraid of a vast new experience, one that had already happened, but which he forestalled acknowledging. He was afraid of being altered, shaken, of having demands placed upon him. He was afraid of being seen as an older man living with a younger one. He was afraid of any experience that would upset the careful plodding order of his life.

"I have so much to *lose*," he said. His hands were clenched into fists.

"And of course nothing to gain," Daniel said stiffly.

Emotion alters vision. The softness of the gardens a moment before now hardened, their secrets closing within themselves when Daniel's imagination and emotion could no longer concentrate on them with pleasure. Mystery became meaningless, one of the many things useless in a shallow world of appearance and calculated deception.

That a man should be forced to regard even the possibility of love as a problem, as something dangerous if made known, was something Daniel refused to accept. Yet he saw the reasons all too clearly. He loved, and for him that was good and necessary. He loved courageously, knowing full well the injunctions placed against his love. He had suffered for loving, and still he would love. But what of the others—James was one of them—who hadn't the sheer force of emotion to carry them along, to make words like courage ridiculous and unnecessary?

Daniel knew what James meant. The check on emotion, on love, was based on the practical side of things. Daniel loathed practicality.

He walked away from James, following a path towards the river. A shimmer of water could be seen through the soft grieving branches of a line of willows. There was a point at which words became meaningless and argument hopeless. He had reached it. Once or twice he looked up, around him, at what had minutes before felt connected to him, a part of something, some hope, within himself. A positive in a beneficient world. Now what he saw existed without him. The world was flat and tedious, filled with negatives in an empty void.

It took him back to his only lover. When he was nineteen he had been in love with a man his own age, Jacob. Jacob could express his love only when, with one drug or another, he could trick his love into believing that the world allowed it. But the drugs had finally tricked Jacob, taken him, sucked him into a nightmare that showed him every day the terrors a mind keeps at bay, a world worse than any his love could have produced.

Daniel stood staring blindly at the river. Perhaps he should return and attempt to discuss things calmly, blotting out his emotion, so that James would not panic. Was more time needed? More patience? And if so, for what purpose? What end, or what beginning? Hadn't they just now faced head-on the central obstacle to further involvement? Daniel had forced it and had seen the stone barrier, the wall, from behind which James answered him. Should he let it go now? Let James go, and with him, a part of himself? Stab once and for all the heart of his love, and hope, and let it slowly drain itself, empty and die?

Or should he fight for James? He knew the weapons he could use, knew the carrying force of his love, its goddamnable persistence. But at what point did force cease to be the universal right of the lover, the lover's blind battling crusade, and become instead self-conscious machinations, maneuvers, a selfish, egocentric use of power?

Daniel didn't know. Being in the vortex of emotion, he was too dizzy to see clearly. He knew that if he pulled out now, withdrew his love, it would in a perverse way let James prove to himself that of course he had been right all along: love between men didn't and couldn't last.

It shouldn't have to be so difficult, he thought bitterly. It shouldn't have to be so conscious. Love should reduce problems by its own generous impulsive force, not create them.

When he turned, there was James, nervously watching him, his face pained.

"I didn't want to hurt you," James said in a low voice. "I didn't want to hurt you when I said that."

"I know you didn't."

"I didn't want to hurt you because you . . . you have never hurt me." He shifted his weight. Daniel said nothing. "You have given me far more than I could ever give to you. And that's not fair, do you see? It's not fair to you."

Daniel turned back to the river.

"I can't be brave in the splendid ways you can be," James said. "At times I want to be but—it's not something I can ignore. Not in my position. Not without tenure in a small private college. I am under scrutiny."

"Their standards are your standards," Daniel said quietly. "You accept them even if they're based on lies and ignorance. Even if they contort you into something you're not. You suffer for them."

James looked at him, his face drawn.

"Perhaps you make them care when in fact they don't, or wouldn't," Daniel said.

"You say that even after what happened with your own family?" James said. "No, you don't know the ruthlessness of academic life. How inhumane the Humanities have become."

"I do know. I see its effect on you every time we're together." Daniel came close to him. He spread his hands. "Things are changing. Slowly. Not fast enough to satisfy me, but they are changing. And we've got to be a part of that. We've got to help make it positive. But you seem to be doing everything you can to prevent change." James was silent.

"You've made me into an issue instead of a person. That's what hurts me. You've put me on their level, and that's a place where I don't want to be. But I've said all this and too much already, and I don't want to say it again. It's too frustrating. I love you."

Something was to be decided here, now, in this garden, with the kind of ridiculous solemnity such moments require. A stillness descended upon them, and outside of it the birds threw their confetti of song.

"Please come to me," James said, and sneezed.

November

1972

Daniel excused himself as he squeezed past several pairs of
stout German knees, careful not to stub any thick nyloned
ankles as he took his excellent seat on the main floor of the
Deutsche Oper, Berlin.

He was thinking of Tilda, how she cried, and how the
glasses she had worn at the airport adjusted their tint according
to the light intensity. Tilda, why couldn't she be here to listen
to his fears and excitements as he always listened to hers?

Of course what he was doing would be incomprehensible to
most of their mutual friends. Most of them would disapprove. In
some ways Daniel himself could not help but disapprove. Love
had always meant to him certain duties—yes, duties, the very
word that he, modern reader, always hated to come across in
Victorian novels. Duty. Cause of so much unhappiness.

Quick to rationalize, to untie the knots, he reminded himself that duties in love had to be reciprocal . . . in real love,
romantic love, which he persisted, despite his modernity, in
believing was possible.

It was easy to be superficially angry with James. James
the unchanging, James the never trying, James, who could

never ease the burden of tension from his intelligent, handsome face. But this anger of Daniel's never struck deep. He was constitutionally unable to remain angry for long. It wasn't worth it. And after living with James for over a year, he knew him well enough to understand the reasons for that unchangeableness, that tension.

Absurdly enough, he still loved James, which was why he could not help but disapprove of what he was doing. On the other hand, there were times when you simply realized that you were exhausted from giving and working to receive.

But all this thinking about it: he'd gone through it over and over again and then some more, and still—here he was, in Berlin.

He flipped through the pages of the program to the cast list for that evening's performance. And there he saw printed, singing the title role, the name Peter Puckett. Pater Pookit, as the Germans said. Daniel flipped to the photograph of the principle singers. There, posed at his best angle, wearing a thoughtful smile, his large dark eyes confident and yet unconfiding, was Peter Puckett, the black American tenor who was singing his first *Tannhäuser.*

This was a new production, but not the first performance. The first few had been sung by a cast much better known than this one, lead singers in the operatic firmament with the price of tickets to hear them appropriately astronomical. Tonight it was because of Puckett and a young Swedish soprano who was to sing both Venus and Elisabeth that there was such an excitement to be felt in the audience of well-dressed Germans.

"*Ein schwarzer Tannhäuser* (A black Tannhäuser)," the stout older woman seated next to Daniel remarked to her husband. "*Ganz fabelhaft, nicht?* (Utterly fabulous, isn't it?)"

"*Amerikaner,*" replied her husband, nodding, pointing to the information beside Puckett's photograph. "*Er kommt aus California.* (He comes from California.)"

Daniel smiled to himself. His hands were shaking slightly

with excitement. What stories for Francis Turner and Dobbin Riggs, if they only knew!

Peter Puckett had been singing with various smaller companies in Germany for three years, primarily the Italian repertory, but he had taken secondary Wagnerian roles in Cologne and Stuttgart. The German press had then singled him out as a young tenor with great promise, perhaps even *Heldentenor* promise. In a country that awaits the heroic tenor as others do the Messiah, this was not an unusual statement for the press to make.

But now, here Peter Puckett was in Berlin, essaying a major and extremely taxing Wagnerian role for the first time, that of the youthful knightly sinner/singer Tannhäuser. People were waiting. And of course a great deal of the interest in him was because he was black (*"ein schwarzer"*), for while there was no end of talented black sopranos and mezzos unknown to American opera houses but well-known in the German, where they had made their reputations, there was definitely an absence—one might say a void—on any major stage of black tenors. And black tenors who sang Wagner (mostly to white women, of course), who were *Heldentenors* (which carried a certain respect in itself), were even rarer than that, and couldn't help but be of interest, even cultural titillation.

Daniel took a few unobtrusive deep breaths to relax himself. He was sitting in a seat obtained for him by Peter Puckett. After tonight's performance he would see Peter Puckett again. He had come to Berlin because of Peter Puckett. And all the while he was thinking of James. There was one face in his restless thoughts: James'.

Applause sprinkled down like a spring shower when the conductor appeared. People arranged themselves, getting out last-minute coughs, closing their programs, quieting. The houselights went down. The conductor raised his baton. The overture began.

Summer

1972

James' brother Loren had come to visit late in the summer
and accompanying him was Peter Puckett. Puckett had,
several years earlier, been a member of Loren's Symphonic
Choir and a private voice student of his at Calistoga College in
Los Angeles. It was, in fact, because of Loren's prompting and
with the help of various musical connections of Loren's that
Puckett, then twenty-eight and teaching high school, had finally been persuaded to make the trip to Germany and audition
for several German opera houses.

Puckett remained in Germany and his return to the States
that summer was his first in nearly five years. Almost more important than seeing this family in Oakland was Puckett's desire to see Loren in Los Angeles. Their reunion had been arranged long beforehand. From Los Angeles they planned to
drive north together, leisurely, along the coastal highway, so
that after the visit with James, whom Puckett had never met,
Puckett could go on to audition for a role in Vancouver.

Puckett was at a crucial point in his career, and since his
career had become, in most respects, his life, he thought he
wanted Loren's advice and support. But five years of erratic

talk by mail is not the same as five years of close personal contact and discussion. Both Loren and Puckett, like the price of
stamps, had changed.

Puckett had not unnaturally become a great deal more ag-
gressive and self-conscious—to the point of affectation some
would say—because of the work he did and his sojourn abroad. It
was, he discovered, difficult to unzip that accreted skin of professional self-consciousness; even, perhaps, slightly demeaning.

He had once been an eager student of Loren's; he had
been a "Negro of Promise"; but now he had matured vocally
and professionally, taken over his own life (with the help of his
manager), filled out in his own ways.

A musician is always a student, if for no other reason than
that there is always new music to be learned. But no longer was
Puckett Loren's student. No longer confiding, excited, eager
to hear advice and criticism and to act on it. Learning was more
in the line of duty and necessity now, and had its application in
a real professional world, a world in which you had to sell what
you had. Puckett found that he was no longer willing or able to
listen and accept everything Loren said. There were many
things he could not tell Loren. Having returned to a point of
reference—California—Puckett was made suddenly aware of
what he had become since leaving it. The old days were no
more.

Puckett had shared something unique with Loren, a special affection. He had had complete confidence in Loren's
musical integrity (that had not changed), and had understood
instantly what Loren was after in his, Puckett's, voice. Now
that old rapport had gone slack. And Puckett missed it. God,
how he missed it.

He missed it especially because he was back in America
and had returned a stranger. Where did he fit in now? His
speech, grown so careful, combed with a light undefinable accent, sounded pretentious and theatrical here. His own family
was awed by him.

He told himself that other things ruled his life now. There were limitations one had to adjust to in one's personal life. As a performer you were of necessity forced to keep a third eye turned on yourself, an eye like a theater spotlight picking you out on stage. The eye of the theater god. Puckett had worked too hard, given up too much, and had come too far to dim that light now. This was no longer a student recital.

And then, too, it was not entirely his fault, this barrier with Loren. Loren was suffering something. Puckett was embarrassed by suffering, it made him nervous and impatient. Since Loren declined to reveal its source, or even to mention it in any way, Puckett had no opportunity to share it, to let this— whatever it was—be a means of *rapprochement* between them.

Each was held tight within himself. Neither was able to step through the walls which time had erected in their friendship. They stood nose to nose, not quite touching, knowing that the other breathed, glad of it, but unable to hear or feel the breath itself. Did this come with age? Was it some peculiar masculine emotional atrophy? Or was it simply and basically human, an inability to drop one's eternally guarded self, to put down the armor of habituated reserve and thereby expose the fragile shrine of bones holding a tender heart?

Earlier that summer, on a fine, clear evening in June, James, Daniel and two guests walked down the central gravel path in the gardens. It had been nearly a year since Daniel moved in.

One of the guests, Professor Karl Fredrickson, was the head of the history department at the college where James taught. The other, Helen Fredrickson, had had the tags "faculty wife" and "gracious hostess" so long embossed upon her, that she appeared to be living in a kind of perpetual society page photograph.

According to photographs, Mrs. Fredrickson was most comfortable pouring tea or martinis in her own gigantic living room in the West Hills, where her gowns, silver tea service and gin could adequately complement the famous vista of mountains to be seen from her windows. She came from one of Portland's oldest and wealthiest families and vicious rumor whispered that her husband had married her for money and connections.

This couple, the Fredricksons, gracefully middle-aged and professional in their marriage, walked side by side down the gravel path with just enough room beside them for James. Daniel had no choice but to follow behind like a geisha. He did so with his hands in his pockets. Because the Fredricksons were not certain where or how to place Daniel, they had subtly excluded him all evening.

Daniel spent hours preparing the meal (he was a much better cook than James was), only to have his work dismissed by a few polite, monotonous comments on the food. His own friends, he reflected, nursing this particular grudge as he walked along, would have been shouting their delight and pleasure.

Daniel hated pinched social talk because nothing was said and its only purpose was to pass time or do business. Their predictable litany of subjects, all related to the college, further excluded him. He would have welcomed some discussion in which he could participate, some inflaming topic that would allow him to argue: Kent state, the invasion of Cambodia, the Pentagon Papers, the anti-war protests shaking colleges and universities throughout America. But conversation remained private, well-bred and stiffly dull.

The Fredricksons were James' guests, and so Daniel had wanted to think of them as his guests as well. They were here because James felt obligated to return the dinner to which they had weeks earlier invited him.

Daniel had no illusions. He knew that even now he would not be invited to their home. That would make him a couple with James. Helen Fredrickson was the sort of hostess who always had a "lady" for every "gentleman"; partners of the same sex were to her an incomprehensible *faux pas*. So Daniel, having no place in this professional scheme of things, would remain invisible, a displaced freak of one evening's duration, to be mildly thanked and immediately forgotten.

For James, the situation was touchy. Social life of this sort was a part of his professional life. Karl Fredrickson was not just a casual friend to have over for dinner. He was a part of the conservative college establishment, that body of fate-dealers for whom impropriety or abnormality were grounds for denying tenure. With one comment, Fredrickson could make James' career precarious. Reason was never used in these cases; reasons were never given. It was something one did not speak about openly, or have to prove.

Why, then, did James have the Fredricksons over, with Daniel so obviously there? Because at some point not even James could tolerate the position he was in. Love had not made him brave, but tonight for him was a small act of courage. He had nearly cancelled the arrangements at the last minute, and had gone so far as to suggest that perhaps, coward that he was, it would be better if Daniel were not there. The look of hurt and incipient fury on Daniel's face quickly prompted James to withdraw the suggestion.

And of course James wanted people to meet Daniel, the person who had made the experience of love real for him. It was just that there would be no problems of any kind if Daniel did not materialize, was not visible, if James did not have to say that Daniel lived there. Daniel had a couple of times already conveniently disappeared so that James could have someone over. Mostly he was left out when James went elsewhere. James never mentioned Daniel in public, no one knew Daniel existed, so how could Daniel ever be asked?

Daniel had thus far and uneasily accepted this, though he was hurt, bitter and angry. James, he knew, had lived with a sense of his own private indignity for so long that by now he almost assumed it to be a natural consequence of homosexuality. Daniel, on the other hand, as he became more active in gay events and politics, was seeing first hand, in his own life, the effects of emotional repression.

Now, in the garden, Mrs. Fredrickson was looking about with a faint curiosity which further irritated Daniel. They were walking through a magnificent garden that he was reclaiming after years of neglect, full of effects and surprises so beautiful to him that he expected others to be as enthusiastic as he was.

"What are those things called, James?" Mrs. Fredrickson asked, nodding her head in the direction of a flowerbed.

"Those? What are those, Dan?" James asked.

"Lupins. Russell lupins," Daniel said, a little sullenly. Mrs. Fredrickson, he noticed in his growing *I vs. them* attitude, hadn't bothered to ask him or even to look at him. And James had made no mention of the fact that he, Daniel, was the one restoring the gardens. This would have been the time to do it, to wedge him into their hard-walled, privileged, academic midst.

Daniel began to actively dislike having them here. They spoiled the romance of the gardens, the glowing mysteries of light, form, colors. They distorted Daniel's vision of what the gardens should be, and made his secret proprietorship a kind of mockery. Who walked in these gardens? Not lovers. "They smell like pepper," he said. "The lupins."

"One wouldn't wish them in the house, then," said Mrs. Fredrickson.

"I put them all over," Daniel said. "They're beautiful in large arrangements."

"Strange flowers," replied Mrs. Fredrickson, ending the exchange.

"Daniel has been doing all the gardening work," James said.

Daniel's heart flamed. He was proud of James.

"Lucky you," said Mrs. Fredrickson with a stiff little laugh. "People who can cook and garden are so difficult to find these days."

Daniel's mouth opened but a sudden pleading look from James closed it again.

"That's quite an output of roses," said Mr. Fredrickson, nodding towards a flaming trellis of Provence roses.

"It's in the pruning and the manure," Daniel said. "You know how it is with roses. You can never give them too much shit."

They walked on, and to Daniel's amazement he saw that the gardens really did bore them. Or perhaps it was that they bored one another. For a moment, looking at Mrs. Fredrickson's stiff, styled hair and carefully made-up face, and Mr. Fredrickson's expensive, fitted suit, and their zestless, slow, careful walk, Daniel felt something like sympathy for them. He wondered if they had guessed about him and James.

A soft gallop was heard behind them, and Sylvie came dashing up, grinning, loose hairs flying. "Have you been exploring?" Daniel asked, patting her head. Sylvie shook herself enthusiastically, more loose hairs flying.

"Is it a recognized breed?" Mrs. Fredrickson asked.

"Half breed," Daniel said. "Spaniel and setter. I recognize it."

Some of Sylvie's perennially shedding hair floated over to settle on Mrs. Fredrickson's dark blue skirt and jacket. She gave her sleeves a brush and said, "Pretty dog," through a wan smile.

They had turned to resume their walk when Pepper, Tilda's runty tomcat, poked through a laurel hedge and regarded the four humans with wide eyes and wobbling head. Daniel was keeping the cat for Tilda, who was staying in New York following her impending divorce. Tilda had nursed Pepper through the distemper which left him sweet-natured and blissful in an idiotic sort of way, as well as unusually clumsy. The cat had occasional *petite mal* fits and fell asleep every night noisily sucking it's paw.

Now, thinking that he would dash out and skitter past them, Pepper emerged from the laurel—fast was very slow for him—but tripped on a branch and fell over. Pepper's gait was somewhat grotesque because of the damage done to his motor coordination. He walked sideways, the back of his body never following directly behind the front, but hurrying to walk beside it. Daniel noticed that James and the Fredricksons had stopped, fascinated, to watch.

Sylvie loved cats and always had. She and Pepper got along very well. Pleased to see her friend, Sylvie now ran over with a smile and sniffed. Pepper crouched low to the ground and gave a welcoming mew. Sylvie, grinning, assumed a male copulating position and merrily began to hump Pepper's back.

Daniel burst into laughter. "Talk about natural inversion!" he said.

The Fredricksons, bewildered and embarrassed, turned away. For their benefit James said, "Sylvie, stop that!" and looked at Daniel with a tense face. Daniel tried to hold back his laughter. James smiled quickly, furtively, and turned back to his guests with a loud sneeze.

"Do you suffer from allergies too?" Mrs. Fredrickson asked sympathetically, and when James nodded, continued, "So do we, right down the line. Karl, myself, Janie, Jackie and Joseph too. Of course we all have our shots every year and our various medications. We are all halfway normal now through the summer months, compared to what we used to be."

"It's only on certain days, certain kinds of days that I'm bothered," James said.

"And of course half of it's psychological," Daniel added.

"Usually very dry," James said quickly, "with a hot eastern wind. Or a sudden drop or rise in the barometric pressure."

"I'm sure there are many things here in this garden which increase your misery," Mrs. Fredrickson said soothingly. "You never know what it might be. We all had our extensive tests, of course. Jackie is allergic to roses, of all things. All of us to animal hair."

"Sylvie, walk back here with me; heel," Daniel said. Sylvie had left off humping Pepper and was now walking slightly ahead of Mrs. Fredrickson, banging her tail against Mrs. Fredrickson's knee.

"Oh, it's all right," Mrs. Fredrickson said. "I've had my series already this year, so I can breathe. One never will adjust to cigarette smoke, though." She sighed.

Daniel had lit a cigarette after dinner, carefully waiting until every morsel of food had been consumed and then standing by the French doors with his cigarette held outside and his exhalations pointed in that direction.

Mrs. Fredrickson further elaborated on the various allergies that had at one time, before science eradicated the worst reactions, beset herself, her husband and their three children.

"I've never been bothered in that way," Daniel said from behind them. "I don't think there's a single thing I'm allergic to."

"You're very lucky," Mrs. Fredrickson replied, "but we are all allergic to something. You simply haven't found yours yet. Something somewhere is just waiting to inflame your sinuses and make your eyes itch and your throat tickle."

"I can't think of what it would be," Daniel said, surreptitiously pinching James. "Let's go down this path," he said, turning off from the main axis and now in the lead. "There are some beautiful things blooming this way."

Obediently they turned and proceeded single-file (Indian-fashion, Daniel thought to himself, silently laughing at the notion of the Fredricksons in buckskin) until Mrs. Fredrickson stopped and pointed and said: "Look at those queer things. What on earth are they?"

"Which queer things?" Daniel asked.

"Those," she said, pointing.

They were all silent, knowing that Daniel was the one who had to answer.

"The vulgar name is Red-Hot poker, or Torch Lily. *Doryanthea excelsa*," he said. "You know, every time I look at them I think of Edward the Second."

"Edward the Second?" Mr. Fredrickson said, turning around. He taught British history. "Why Edward the Second?"

"Because of the way he was put to death, of course," Daniel said.

Mrs. Fredrickson was silent for a moment, trying to remember. "Was he . . . burned?" she asked.

"No, dear," said her husband.

Daniel crossed his arms. "Because he was a homosexual they took red-hot pokers and shoved them up his asshole. Poor man, can you imagine?"

James sneezed once, twice, three, four times in quick succession, looking at Daniel between his explosions. Mrs. Fredrickson didn't seem particularly perturbed by this revelation. She said nothing, but did turn to look again at the tall, gaudy, sinister plumes glowing like torches.

"Now we can't judge one barbarous act as exceptional in an age filled with commonplace barbarism and cruelty," Professor Fredrickson said. "And certainly we can't make Edward himself into any kind of martyr when we examine some of his own acts—"

He was about to continue when a tiny, barely fledged bird suddenly dropped like a soft stone in front of them, thudding on the path. A shrill nervous chatter started up in an old Gravenstein apple tree spreading high above and a robin swooped down trying to frighten them away. Stunned, the baby bird lay still. They all stared. Its feathers were thin and oily-looking and its tiny breast pumped hard and fast. With a peep it opened one tiny black eye and tried to move, tried to do something in this hard alien environment into which it had fallen.

"Poor little thing," Daniel said, slowly approaching it. "I'm going to try to nurse it."

Sylvie, who had been nosing nearby, turned just then and she, too, saw the bird struggling on the path. Either her ancient hunting sense flared or she mistook it for a bit of tasty garbage: she dashed over, scooped the bird up in her mouth, and made off with it. The bird, bound in the prison bars of her teeth, kept up a pathetic peeping.

"Sylvie, drop it! Drop it, I said!" Daniel shouted, running after her. But by then the ghastly shock of entry into the new world had so terrified the bird that it died.

The Fredricksons left not long after—the house, that is, not the world.

He was out wandering in the garden again. James, on the way to his study with a glass of iced tea, caught sight of him through the four long windows that formed a floor-to-ceiling bay at one end of the first floor hallway.

Daniel looked haunted somehow. He passed back and forth in his long cotton robe, feet bare—a postulant, a priest, unable to dream or meditate or rest until he had solved some worldly or spiritual problem. Or a character in a 19th century opera, waiting for a secret lover in an Italian garden.

Tonight he was not working in the garden, as he did many nights, but surveying what he had done and what he still needed to do. Under his robe he would be naked, and a comfortable erotic fantasy played itself out in James' imagination. How tall and dark Daniel looked. The sun had bronzed him, made his shaggy hair rough gold.

Back and forth he walked among the flowers and herbs

planted in the kitchen garden. Occasionally he stopped and pulled a flowerhead to his nose, sampling a smell. The setting sun spun an intense red-orange light across the grass and into the deeper parts of the gardens, lancing through the leaves, flowing thickly around trees, seeping through dense-leaved foliage, glowing on the trunks of the birches.

In the darkening hallway, James held the cold wet glass of tea to his cheek and stared out through the windows at the scene, at the light, at the person in the light. What? What more could he want? More than this would be too much, undeserved. Something in him struggled for words, secret words which had no place in his daily thoughts or work. Something else, simpler, as intense as the falling light, was content simply to glow so deeply in him that it hurt. He did not want to move, only to stare and savor this enormous swelling of . . . satisfaction. He stood transfixed within the mysteries of love.

It was hot and still mid-summer. James had always loved the warm, melancholic peace of summer. But now summer, and all the seasons, had become little more than a series of glimpses and sounds through windows: quick images he had to savor and enjoy quickly, compressing them to a remembered essence. A bird darting away. A cloud. The color of a leaf. His work demanded more and more of his time, of his life, of his feelings. When he saw Daniel, as often as not it was like this, through a window, before the discipline of his work directed him to office or study. He was blotting out his private life so that the directed rigors of his professional one could continue without disruption.

This work was research for his first book, and upon its completion and publication his tenure at the college would depend. Any published work was looked upon favorably; more favorably than classroom performance. There was intellectual satisfaction in his work, of course but the satisfaction would have been far greater, and the pressure far less, had James not known just how much, professionally, depended upon it.

But he also knew that the pressure he put on himself to work such long long hours came undeniably from a wish to avoid Daniel. How could this be so? He felt a sudden, sharp fear that some tangled, emotional misalignment in his psyche was dooming him to appreciate life only when it was on the other side of a window.

Where did this new ridiculous fear come from? How could he love someone and at the same time be afraid of him? James felt then, standing in the hallway and looking out at the person he loved, all the inadequacies of his emotional life. He loved, but could not speak. He depended upon a kind of magic telepathic knowledge between himself and Daniel—but he did not believe in telepathy.

Love was a question of freedoms within an encompassing boundary. The boundary had to remain elastic and durable if love was to survive. Love was not a dead carcass, a dead land where people hid themselves away and peeked longingly out of windows at people they loved. James knew this. He knew that if people like the Fredricksons chose to see Daniel as tauntingly vulgar, it did not mean that Daniel was so. And yet people like the Fredricksons, in the end, were the ones who made James sometimes think that he should give Daniel up. It was for the sake of people like the Fredricksons that James remained afraid of Daniel, of their life together, that made James always walk on tiptoe lest he disturb their fragile notions of propriety.

Love hadn't made him brave in his feelings about himself. He had made "that part" of his life a doomed tragedy which he refused to let even love redeem. It was the great embarrassment, the disfiguring wart.

But love in its industrious, busy way had worked some changes in James. He was not always sunk in a puddle of despondent, hopeless gloom. In the mornings, when Daniel got up and went naked to the window to look out at the gardens, and then returned to bed for a few minutes beside him, James felt a frightfully intense sense of rightness, a tenderness elbowing its way into his usual morning torpor.

They slept in the bedroom that had been his parents'. For a few nights after they first moved in, James' dreams had been grueling, vivid, ghastly, as if a hot brand were being applied to tender parts of his subconscious. He remembered fragments of the dreams, something new for him, and was persuaded by Daniel to divulge them.

Progress. Daniel talked about the progress of a life. The need to accept oneself despite deep social prohibitions to do so. And it did seem that Daniel's life moved forward, matured visibly. Maturity to James had always meant the full expression of one's capabilities: the achievement, the ripe reachable fruit that was one's reward for hard, disciplined work. Intellectually he was reaching this point. Emotionally he was not.

Perhaps he could not? And perhaps this was where love would always remain a failure, striking arrows furiously, savagely, into a heart that had to remain quiet and docile, a good boy, instead of making that heart cry out with the joy, wonder and pleasure of each stabbing thrust.

Here James felt that he was a hindrance to Daniel. Daniel vocalized his love, made it visible and real with words and gestures and acts; he took his love out and examined it, played with it, laughed with it. James might look on with skeptical delight but he was, generally, too self-conscious to respond in kind. Even in his own home—their own home. The drowsy, watching spell had not been broken.

So that Daniel, he could see, slowly withdrew his exuberance, patted it into shape, tamed it by denying its expression. But when he did this, he was no longer Daniel, but rather a dulled version of him.

Almost a year of living together. How different already from the first surge of blinding emotion. There was a period

when this emotion seemed to carry James along without allowing for any guidance. The suck and roll of the wave took James
in and showed him its fierce natural power.

One night in a never-to-be-repeated-or-forgotten fit of
romantic ecstasy and longing, James had driven to Daniel's
apartment building in the middle of the night. He had climbed
up the tree growing outside the room where Daniel (and
sometimes James with him) slept. The shades were up and the
windows open to let in a breeze. The church across the street
looked on with a benign calm. James looked in at Daniel sleeping, naked amidst a Baroque tangle of sheets, and felt all the
brittle lines of his being dissolve. An immense and indefinable
relief made him feel weightless and delightfully absurd—as
if, having left the burden of his usual consciousness on the
ground, he could now float in the joys of a new one that left him
a free man instead of a prisoner.

Sylvie growled and barked once when James tapped softly
on the window. Daniel sprang out of bed and stood looking con-
fusedly around the room. When he saw James his face grew
bright and solemn.

"I've come," James said, his heart pounding, "to carry
you away."

"I'm ready to go," Daniel said, helping James in.

Daniel's mouth was fiercely on his, and James' hands
were pressing Daniel's sleep-warm flesh. James' clothes were
off in a second and he and Daniel were on the bed, making
love, all of this passing in a kind of intense, wide-awake dream
they both shared.

But now the old familiar tension, the call of duty. The tabs
of his alphabetical reference file rose in his mind like tiny frantic accusations: A! B! C! An image of his unfinished
work for the day, his stacked desk, his papers, letters, books
index cards, all rose to swallow the memory of a year past. If
James did not push back every day the accumulation of his
work, like a mounting wave it would finally crash over him. He

saw towers of loose papers, stacked and swaying perilously. His study and office he regarded as havens from emotion, but they nonetheless exerted a power over him that was not purely intellectual.

And here he tried to force his vision to rise above the haggard academic depths where so often it was impaled and give himself a few seconds more to look at Daniel in the garden.

The slanting light sprayed the flowers with fever, making the petals throb. The birds let drop cool, soft, quiet notes. The faint rhythmic burr of crickets rose from dry grassy places. And there, just beyond the glass, was Daniel. Daniel in the garden, among the leaves and flowers and light and scent.

The light thickened, ripened, lay still in a climax. Daniel stood without moving, staring at something. James left the vision like that and padded through the warm twilight in the house to his study, his work.

"Tilda, do you think love—"

"All the time, sweetie, for all the fucking good it does me."

Daniel pulled the soft lobe of her ear. Tilda had been a different person since her divorce, and she was only now starting to come back to herself. She had been utterly drained of energy, sapped like the victim of a vampire. Some emotional nerve had been severely pinched, flattening the depth of the world around her. Her back went out. Her skin lost its glow, turning pale and flaccid. She dragged around a miserable carcass.

Daniel and other friends urged her to get away for a month or two, go back to New York to visit family and old friends. Tilda was hesitant but finally talked into it. She hated every minute of New York, but it had the effect of snapped fingers in the face of a hypnotic. She started to come alive again.

She and Daniel were sitting on a stone bench tucked away in an intimate, particularly romantic corner of the garden.

Behind them rose a laurel hedge with species roses festooned among its branches. Nearby, the crowded spires of an old bed of foxglove rose up in a drenching summer light.

"No, listen to me," Daniel said. "We're two characters in this novel, you see, and we're sitting here in the Paradise Gardens, in the summer, talking. Bees are droning and drinking—"

"Sucking," Tilda said.

"—and so on. Description of sun on flowers if you like. And I turn seriously to you, Tildy, and say—"

" 'Tilda, do you think love—' "

"Yeah, do you think it reaches a plateau or some kind of stopping place?"

"If you want it to," Tilda said.

"But love's an active force, isn't it? I mean it's alive somehow, if we let it be. It's positive."

"Until it becomes negative," Tilda said.

"That's what I mean. Is it limited somehow, our capacity to love? Because people are?"

"Are what?"

"Limited. And then should we accept that limitation and be content with it? Assuming two imperfect individuals are involved."

"If two perfect individuals were involved, my dear, would they need love? All it does is make the imperfect seem perfect. It's all a goddamned illusion."

Daniel said nothing.

"Pour me some more lemonade. Then I must fly back to my hot bachelorette pad."

"The Gay Divorcee."

"Don't I wish," Tilda said with a sigh. "Unattached female. Party Girl. Swinging Single. Why do they all sound so awful?" She looked at Daniel with tears in her eyes. "I'm afraid you're going to ask my advice or something. And really, darling, I don't have any to give." Her face grew soft and she reached over to pull him close. "Oh darling, what *is* wrong?"

Daniel pressed her waist with his hands, and then drew back to look at her. Tilda laughed at her own emotion before beginning to weep again. "Oh," she shuddered, waving a hanky, "why *not* cry? Cry for everybody. Cry for all of us, like a big fat *Mater Dolorosa*. It's a chain reaction with me. And I've just–just–been waiting for the right excuse. It feels good!" she sobbed. "And I still miss that asshole Brenner. I just have–haven't adjusted to being on my own yet. But I will. Goddamn it, I will!" With a loud sniff she drew herself up until she was sitting primly with her hands clasped in her lap and her ankles crossed. Her body kept shuddering with the effort of crying and wide wet swathes of tears dripped from behind her tinted glasses. "Hug me again, would you?" she asked.

"Tildy, I love you."

"I–I love you-ou-ou. Oh God!" she shrieked when Daniel, thinking to comfort her, began stroking her side.

"What?"

"That turns me on—I'm so sensitive there."

"Should I stop?" Daniel asked.

"Yes—no—since we're not going to fuck, no. Oh Daniel, I haven't fucked for—God, it seems like months. I can't stand it. I'm in a state of—"

"Tension?" he offered.

"No—yes, that too. No—complete readiness. It's terrible. I'm turned on all the time lately. But I still fan-fantasize about making it with Brenner." She sniffed. "After all I've gone through with that jerk!"

Daniel lay down on the grass beside the bench.

"Why do you have to be so fucking beautiful?" Tilda said inexplicably before blowing her nose. "I'm sorry, my dear. We've been through my crises a million times and just when you were going to tell me yours—I'm sorry, darling, tell me now."

"It'll sound anti-climactic."

"I know it has something to do with James. I've sensed that for quite a while, you know, even before I left for New York. Are you fighting?"

"We never fight," Daniel said.

"Oh yes, that was Brenner and me. You think fighting is vulgar."

"I don't believe in fighting."

"You fought to get James."

"That was love," Daniel said. "And he fought for me, too. It was harder for him, much harder. But that night he climbed up the tree, you know, and tapped on my window—that's when I knew he really did want me."

"Christ!" She danced for a moment on the brink of another weeping fit. "You haven't fallen out of love with James, have you? *That's* not it."

"No, we love one another."

"Then what for Christ's sake is it? I'm always so afraid that when something happens to me it will automatically happen to you too."

"It's a question of how much," Daniel said.

"How much what, for the sweet love of Christ?"

"Love. How much love. James seems to be imposing some sort of limit on it. It's all just standing still."

"Darling, at least it's standing. His work, all of his never-ending unending perfectly boring *work*. My dear, the man is *always* working!"

"It's more than that. Like some large hand in him is always pushing part of me back, never completely accepting me."

"Have you told him this?"

"In various ways. This limit I was talking about. Maybe it's a limit in him and he won't ever be able to go beyond it. If that's the case, I have to learn to live with it."

"Learn to live with it?" Tilda huffed. "Christ, that's the

phrase our mothers used when they found out something they hated about our fathers. That's the crap I got all my life, my dear, and when Brenner was making life hell, sheer fucking unmitigated hell, that was the one goddamn phrase that came to me. Learn to live with it. Why? Learn to live without it would have been better."

Daniel sat up. "Listen to me. I believe that love has certain duties, certain obligations, and no one nowadays wants obligations. I know I'm stupidly old-fashioned, but I think that when you're in love with someone you have to work at it. You have to garden it. You have to have patience and hope for its eventual outcome. You can't always push as hard as you want."

"You just want James to tell you that he loves you, isn't that what this all boils down to?"

Daniel picked a sweet-smelling sprig of mignonette and tucked it into Tilda's bosom. "I think romance can be real. I know it can. You just have to see life as something extraordinary instead of ordinary. And I want James to be a part of this extraordinary world, a part of me, a part of all this." He meant the gardens.

For a moment they sat without speaking in the immense, silent spill of sun. Daniel rose and held out his hand. "Come and I'll show you my new secret."

"How beautiful it is here," Tilda said, wobbling on his arm as she removed her Wedgies. She took his hand and they walked slowly down the central path. "Such a soft romantic jumble. I feel like I should have a little colored parasol—Henry James, or Renoir. It makes me want to start painting again."

"Paradise Gardens," Daniel said.

"What does that mean?"

"It's a kind of English garden. I think James' mother had it in mind when she was designing this garden."

"It looks pretty undesigned to me. More natural than planned."

"That's the point," Daniel said. "It has all these different plant and tree species from every continent in the world, all growing together, here, right here. You'd never find this in nature. But it's been so carefully planned that it looks natural."

"It looks like a dream," Tilda said.

"It is a dream, I suppose. It's the dream of James' mother. She created it. It was her secret paradise. Her Eden. Her vision. And now here I am, trying to get it back for her."

"For her? For *you*," Tilda laughed.

"For all of us," Daniel said. "Come this way—there, in the center, above the pool."

Tilda stared. "How beautiful," she whispered. She broke away and ran across the grass to the newly installed statue. "Beautiful! What is it? What's it's name?"

"Vertumnus. The Roman god of gardens and orchards and changing seasons and all that's pleasant in nature."

"Oh God, he's so handsome," Tilda said. "Is he single? Tell him I'm an easy lay." She walked around the Roman god, carefully examining it. "Darling, this is where I'll paint you. Right here, by Vertumnus. I've got the idea already," she said excitedly. "Right here. I'll paint you in your Paradise Gardens."

"James too?"

"Is he ever out here? I've never seen him."

"If you do a painting of me, I want him to be in it."

"I'll never get him to pose," Tilda said. "I know he won't do it."

"Vertumnus will get him to do it."

"Get Vertumnus to do it for me while you're at it."

"A dip?"

"Absolutely."

Shedding clothes, they talked quietly until they reached the willow trees and the river. The water was dark and deliciously cold. It accepted their bodies with serene indifference.

* * * * * * *

As they made their way up Highway 101, skirting the Pacific, Loren never exceeded the speed limit. Puckett wondered if Loren's old Volkswagen could. Now that he was back on the highways of America Puckett felt an excited urge, almost an instinct, to fly along at great speeds. The eternally fast nation was America, all movement, a nation of heads whizzing past in huge cars and campers on endless wide, well-paved highways, everything along the route geared to speed, formulaic hospitality, instant gratification.

The size of America came back to bewilder and enchant Puckett. He had forgotten how enormous a place it was, and how uncrowded in comparison to Europe. The trip north, from Los Angeles to Portland, with Loren never exceeding the speed limit, was to take at least five days. Where in Central Europe would it take so long to reach a destination?

For the past five years Puckett's world had primarily been the Germany of provincial opera houses. Now that training period (as he thought of it) was soon to end. It had to, for he had told his manager to hold off booking him into smaller houses after next November. Puckett made his Berlin debut then, his Wagnerian debut in a lead role, and he had made that month and that role into the turning point of his career. After that, if he succeeded, the other big houses would be his: Hamburg and Munich, for a start. Vienna in a year. Covent Garden and La Scala in two. And then America, Chicago, San Francisco and the Met.

Driving this long distance was oddly hypnotic. They made few stops during the day and every night pulled into one of the hundreds of anonymous motels lining the coast from San Diego to Tillamook. Loren always took a separate room for himself and shuffled off, after a late supper, to his antiseptic-smelling "unit." After a day spent circumventing his grief, or whatever it was, talking around it—just as Puckett talked around the core of what he really wanted to discuss with his old teacher—Puckett assumed that Loren was retiring to face "it" alone in the garish atmosphere of the motel room.

On one of the nights when Loren was alone in his motel room, Puckett swaddled his neck and went out to walk along the beach. The ocean here was a powerful thing, a particular thing, wild, loud, insistent. Its voice demanded that it be heard.

It was an American ocean, a pioneer ocean, ignoring men and making them feel both tiny and exhilarated. The sight and sound of it had the effect of pummelling a brain into feeling more than thinking.

And Puckett felt. He felt oddly anonymous, for one thing. Ordinary people he would never know, who would never hear of him, or care to, lived in this small coastal town. The smallness of their lives, lives that Puckett saw as little more than an accumulation of inconsequential details, had a suffocating effect on him. How engulfing anonymity was! Puckett thought of his years of study, his memorization of scores, his daily vocal exercises, his learning of German, Italian and French. He tried to put all this into some sort of relation to the people who lived in this shack-ridden American town. What had he to do with them?

In another sense the anonymity was refreshing. Here he could be himself, could be nothing, if he wanted . . . although Puckett was no longer accustomed to thinking of himself as nothing. That, in fact, was dangerous, an insult to his ripening vanity. He now had a fear of being ignored, and ignored he would have been had he not worked twice as hard as the others to reach an even professional footing with them. He had had to work hard to make himself more than a novel curiosity.

Tannhäuser in Berlin in November. That, even now, was assuming terrific importance in his plans for the future. The attainment of the top of the rickety, rotting steps he so often climbed in his dreams. From there a new vista presented itself, waited for him. From this first peak he could dive into the air of fame, and fly. Or fall . . . but no, he would not fall. His voice did have the power and stamina for Wagner, despite Loren's disapproving insistence that it did not. His Berlin debut could never be that disastrous, except in his dreams.

That night Puckett met a young man walking his dog along the beach, and eventually he went home with him. Puckett said he was a salesman. But where, the young man wanted to know, did he pick up that accent? And did being a salesman account for Puckett's . . . well, conservative appearance? The young man thought Puckett would look much better with a huge Afro and—to be honest—if he lost some weight. Didn't smoke? Not even a little grass? If he didn't like hard rock, what kind of music did he like? Opera? The young man thought he had heard of it: wasn't it fat women with antlers on their heads, shouting? Yes, Puckett said, that was exactly what it was.

He left the young man's psychedelic apartment depressed and a little shaken. As he walked back along the beach towards the anonymous motel, he saw in his mind, for some reason, the sanitized glass wrapped in a paper bag in the bathroom. By this time it was dark and the air was thick with mist. To one side of Puckett the sea crashed and roared, but he could not see it.

What kind of world was this, so unreal, phantom, booming? And why on a stage did just that make sense to him, as he sang dialogue over an orchestra, dressed in odd costumes, sweating and swearing vocal love to creatures of the same strange world? The ocean, too, was a kind of orchestra, but before it Puckett could not sing.

He worried lest the damp chill air harm his throat and pulled his silk neck scarf over his mouth and nose. Walking along, muffled, a black man, he felt he must surely look suspicious to anyone from the town. The brief sexual escapade with the young man seemed full of meaning because it had no meaning at all. There had been no real contact. In this atmosphere of mist and darkness the mind of the old, the anonymous Puckett stirred.

It was most curious. As he walked along the beach he felt his connections with the world dissolving. Infinitely remote became the reality of any opera stage on which he made his living and name. Infinitely remote and absurd the whole idea of fame.

The sea thundered, rethundered, a sound dimly in his consciousness for three days now. He took step after step, not knowing where he was walking. Was this the total anonymity he thought might be refreshing? This blind walking, blood and self crammed into moveable limbs? He was anonymous here not only to the world, but to himself. Lonely. Alone.

Next November he would sing *Tannhäuser* in Berlin. But what more? Something in him asked what more there was to Peter Puckett?

Music, music was in him. The sea, ancient, moving, enormous, said, I am the music. Puckett felt as the drowning man must when his fingers slip away from the overturned lifeboat. For a moment he was pulled, not away from consciousness, but more fully into it. For a moment he was centered in it, just as it was. For a moment he felt that everything in him had been creeping around the periphery of this vast, strange, unknowable essence of life.

The fog softly imprisoned him. Puckett sat down in the damp sand and listened to the singing sea. It comforted him. He answered in his own voice, humming a tune like a father rocking a cradle.

In Portland the sky for days had been vast, clear and hot,

proclaiming the final round of summer. Then came several days when the region was prey to "atmospheric disturbances" (a wonderful title for a book, as Daniel pointed out). Dust and pollen blown by storms in the eastern half of the state rode a burning witchy wind down the Columbia Gorge and promptly took up gritty residence on skin and teeth, up noses and down throats. Dobbin Riggs, who had recently returned from Morocco, said it was like a North African sirocco.

James was in an agony, his body reacting to this weather as though it were a minor case of demonic possession. The bed heaved with his sneezes and grunts, which were attempts to draw full breath. His face altered, dripping and itching, and his eyes became burning bits of vision between puffed lids.

Daniel's throat burned; his contact lenses felt like razor blades. He became silent, morose, cranky. Life itself seemed unreasonable, small problems insurmountable.

There were forest fires and fires from fields being cleared, and the smoke from both flowed on the air currents to meet the dust and pollen in Portland. The skies went flat. Fearful, portentous visions in the sky seemed not only possible but imminent—blazing legions of fighting angels, say, like those seen by entire towns in the Middle Ages: heavenly hosts with fiery avenging swords and shields and banners inscribed with divinely unequivocable symbols.

The soil instantly sucked up whatever hosed water was given to it, but most of the water evaporated before it could be of use. Then came a sudden drought emergency. The flowering plants waved their withered, dusty leaves and blossoms in a pathetic transformation. They began to resemble faded stage scenery.

Until finally, in the night, came a sudden, cleansing, violent storm. Thunder cracks throttled the frames of bodies and buildings. Pure clear sea winds erased the dust. Fat chilled drops of rain washed the atmospheric debris into a delighted, guzzling earth.

James and Daniel were sitting out on the terrace the following morning, the world resurrected around them. The light was clear, the sky liquid. A giddy green fragrance swelled the breezes. Once again the birds were singing. They danced down to collect fat, sodden earthworms and noisily bathed in light-flecked pools of water. Those flowers not blown over in the storm stretched themselves on their rejuvenated stalks. Everything living sucked up the sweetness of the morning.

Over his morning paper James said: "We have to decide on the sleeping arrangements for my brother and his friend. They'll be here tonight or tomorrow and we have to get the rooms ready."

Daniel was leaning back in his chair, taking deep breaths. "Easy enough. Loren can have the guest room, his old room, and his friend can sleep with him or use the sofa-bed in your old room."

"I hardly think they'd want to sleep with one another," James said.

"Aren't they lovers?"

"Of course not."

"From everything you've told me about Loren it sounds to me as though he's gay. You wonder about it yourself. How can you not know something like that about your own brother?"

"We're not that close, I told you. It doesn't matter anyway."

"Of course it matters," Daniel said.

"Anyway," James said, snapping his newspaper, "where are you going to sleep?"

Startled, Daniel sat up. "What do you mean, where? I'll sleep where I always sleep, with you!"

James smiled nervously. "I don't think I'm ready for that yet."

Daniel, as if the atmospheric pollution had descended to cling suffocatingly in the air again, was suddenly furious.

"Then make yourself ready!" he shouted. "We have lived together, slept together, for over a year now, and if after all that time you've come out of it with nothing changed, with that same old fucking guilt . . . goddamn it! If after all this time I mean so little to you that you'd actually hide me away in another bedroom—" Rage and the sense of insult made him incoherent.

"I know it sounds awful," James said quietly. "But—"

"But nothing. You just stabbed me, right in the heart."

James reached over and put a hand on Daniel's arm. Daniel shook it off. "Sorry, but I can't be sympathetic. Not this time. I've never said anything when your Aunt Ellen and your Uncle Patrick come and I have to take my pillow and pretend I sleep in another room. I can understand that, even if it stinks on principle." He fixed James with a wide-eyed stare. "But look, a change has to come sometime. You're denying me. You're still trying to sweep me under the rug. And I just won't fit there."

They stared at one another.

"If all of these friends and relatives of yours are going to be so bloody shocked, it's their problem," Daniel said, "no matter how uncompromising it sounds. And that's where change comes in, when people can see that you're still you, you may be gay but you're still you. Christ, did I have to go through all that shit with my family just so I could find out that my lover also thinks there's something wrong with two men being in love?"

James sat half-stunned. All this was not unlike having raw voltage pour in through his unsuspecting ears. When Daniel physically indicated that he was finished, locking his fingers together and banging his elbows on the table to form a canopy over his eyes, James let out a brief, exhausted-sounding grunt. He stared at nothing. He saw his innocent coffee cup and heard meaningless birdsong. His thoughts had scattered, run to hide.

Daniel put a hand on his arm. "This is how people lose one another," he said. "It's more difficult for us if you keep insisting that They are somehow right and We are somehow wrong."

James took his arm away.

"Being in love shouldn't be a struggle," Daniel said. "It shouldn't be political. But right now, for us, it is. In some ways it has to be."

"You preach," James said, his voice dull.

"You need to be preached to."

"You simplify things until there's no possible solution but your solution."

Daniel banged the table with his fist. "When has any solution of mine not been in favor of you or me or anyone, and not positive, and not for what was good?"

"Good is a relative term," said James.

"Look, I'm not preaching any doctrine of hate, even if it's preached against me. Obviously you'll never defend yourself."

James could not believe that he was hearing his own voice making an excuse which even to him sounded lame and despicable. "I have to go in and work." He rose from the table.

"James—" Daniel looked up at him. "I belong here. Don't chase me off the land."

James put his newspaper under his arm and left Daniel sitting alone.

That evening at twilight Puckett stepped out from two open French doors onto a fan-shaped brick terrace. It reminded him instantly of a stage, a strange little stage set up within an enchanted garden—Klingsor's in *Parsifal*, perhaps, or the one in Dvorak's *Rusalka*. On a tiny stage in a small provincial town in Germany, with an embarrassment of an orchestra, Puckett had once sung the role of the Prince in *Rusalka*. The best thing about the production, besides himself, was the soprano's aria, "O Silver Moon," in which Rusalka called upon the moon to light the way for a lover. The soprano's voice turned creamy and full as she sang, and touched Puckett like a spell.

Now a spacious darkening garden spread out around and beyond him. Puckett could see no water, but he could smell it. There was a soft scented breeze.

The flowers beyond the terrace, with a blanket of shadow creeping along the beds and up among the stems, rose in proud, serene outline. A vast, clear, silent late summer sky, deepening its pitch of color, held a silver slice of moon. In the distance the massed trees were black, already heavy with sleep. Crickets rasped a rhythmic tranquility adding to the stillness. Puckett heard a whirr close to his ears, the vibrating wings of bird or insect, he could not tell which.

He had left Loren inside with his brother, so that they could have a few minutes alone. But now he could see a tall, indistinct figure standing on one side of a garden path, surrounded by the dark shapes of flowers and shrubs. Was this James' "friend"?

The outline of the figure grew less and less distinct as the garden slipped fully into its summer darkness. Still it had not moved. Puckett thought he heard a voice, a faint humming, the kind of unconscious lullaby a person uses when alone. His sense of displacement grew. He stood in the oddness of a dream landscape in which nothing can be clearly, with hard vision, seen and grasped.

But now the figure did move and slowly walked down the path towards him. He could hear now that the sound was humming. When it ceased, Puckett knew that he had been seen. The figure neither hurried nor slowed, but kept its same leisurely pace. Stopping, the figure bent over. A rustling sound and a dim snap were heard before the figure straightened and advanced.

"Peter Puckett, I presume?" the figure said, and before Puckett could reply or extend his hand, the man had opened Puckett's shirt pocket and stuck into it a spicy-smelling flower.

The Germans were forever shaking hands, and without this ritual introductions now seemed incomplete to Puckett. "Yes, how do you do?" he said, thrusting out his hand.

"Daniel Hartman," the person said, taking Puckett's hand.

"This is your garden?"

"Ours," Daniel said. "Want to look around?"

"It's rather dark, isn't it?" Puckett, who was never uncertain or shy, now stood shy and uncertain with Daniel Hartman. Of course one's meetings were usually in lighted rooms, not in the night like this.

"There's a way to see a garden at night, too," Daniel said. "By smell. You sort of sniff your way through. And there is a bit of moon."

"What were you humming?" Puckett asked as he stepped out into the darkness. "It sounded familiar, but I couldn't quite hear it."

"I don't remember what it's called," Daniel said. "It's something I heard at a friend's house. It's from an opera."

"Hum just a few bars so I can hear it," Puckett said.

Daniel laughed, then hummed the tune.

"I'll be goddamned," said Puckett.

"What?"

"'O Silver Moon.'"

"Is that what it's called?" Daniel asked.

Puckett's laughter was deep and low, a kind of secret.

"God, that sounds good!" Daniel said, leading him further into the scented darkness of the gardens. Stars began to glow and sparkle above them. "I like the sound of laughter out here."

* * * * * * *

Scratching his pre-eminently scratchable beard, Loren Donahue lay on the bed of his youth in the house of his childhood. He lay on the bed that had never seemed merely a bed. A massive mahogany frame with a high headboard and tall posts in which flowers, fruits, even a strange little face or two were carved, this childhood bed had assumed a personality as Loren grew to know and fill it. It became a kindly, avuncular person who never minded being climbed on or hidden under, and who could be a ship, a palace, a tent, a great unnamed beast, even an entire piano, letting Loren live inside of it and hear as much music as he wanted.

How many nights had he lain in it in the darkness of this room, wondering what sorts of magic places were hiding beneath, half-willing it to rise into the air, squeeze its bulk out through the window, and fly off into a cold starry night with its friend Loren?

The old bed no longer seemed quite so massive. Like his life, it had shrunk. Its livingness was quiet, no longer accustomed to playing games, and it now observed its old occupant with benignity and patience.

It was too warm for the blanket, so Loren's long naked body lay stretched in variations of the basic tortured positions known by heart to insomniacs. Sleep, sleep, how he sought it still, after looking for it for so many years. Sleep took on a meaning when you lost its natural mindless comfort, lost the oblivion of its dark pulling arms. Loren thought of it during the day as he would a waiting lover, and hoped for it at night, fearing that it would not come, half-dreading the judgment that would make itself known when he lay down.

Sleep was aloof, alive, somewhere outside of him rather than inside. The fatal separation. How to coax it, amuse it into being kind? What presents to offer this fickle lover? The night passed, and others slept in it. Those cursed hours were for most people a time of rejuvenation, of strange important dreams . . . and only Loren, the insomniac, was awake, hearing and thinking and feeling all that the night and sleep should have muffled. Consciousness in a huge night sea of unconsciousness, and yet no revelations came. Brünhilde was magicked asleep, but Loren was magicked awake, an antithesis of Sleeping Beauty.

The moon, another friend of his youth, he could see through the branches of the mountain ash. It hung like a slim cruel smile in a freckle of stars. An owl hooted—hooted again—a sound for the sleepless. Loren felt the familiar symptoms in his throat and eyes and gave himself up to another fit of weeping, hoping that it would exhaust him. With a groping, childish motion he reached down to draw the top sheet over him. Weeping felt less lonely when he was covered. Weeping naked and uncovered seemed to signal some kind of symbolic defeat.

So long as the tears continued to drip down around his ears and into his shock of graying hair, he could lay in comparatively dumb relief. This state was infinitely preferable to the prolonged mental tortures that preceded it. So long as *he* lived there, no need to worry about the drought in California, he thought, gloomily amused.

Crying helped to lift a corner of the hot blanket of emotional oppression which had bound him so tight these past weeks. During the daylight hours, and in the company of other people, he was forced to control the latent obscenity of his emotions. Obscene, he called them, because they threatened to knock the equilibrium out of his ordinary, everyday life.

During the day he still had resistance. At night, alone, he must face them, face the magnified, grotesque angles of consciousness. Loren did this wearily, patiently, hoping only that finally this wound, or whatever it was, would heal and leave him in a kind of blind peace. A peace not unlike sleep. It was a depressive cycle he was going through, he told himself, and eventually the cycle must reach its end, dropping him back in line with the old Loren, letting him be whole and healed once more.

A student of Loren's, a young man he had been grooming not unlike Puckett several years earlier, had recently left Loren's tutelage, left a potential career. It was, as far as Loren was concerned, a kind of death, one that was ludicrous and disgusting, slicing this young man in an instant clean away from the musical life flowering ahead of him, of them both.

Alex was his name, and he had a voice given to few men. It immediately struck and subtly moved the listener. It was a voice that could achieve emotional responses with tenderness and intelligent sensitivity rather than relying on swaggering, hard-edged volume. It was not a large voice, as Puckett's had been large. It was a voice for expressive song, and not one for the raging bluster of Grand Opera. It was a haunting voice, just as Puckett's was haunting, but with a much smoother timbre. And as he had loved Puckett's voice, Loren loved this voice, and the man it belonged to.

Loved him still, he supposed, whatever love was. And yet had to consider him as dead and removed from the realm of physical possibility. This was the emotional coupling Loren's mind wove and rewove. Separation, permanent separation, was a death. He, Loren, was mortal. He, Loren, would die. He had already lived over two-thirds of his life. Dreary facts of this kind thudded regularly into his consciousness.

What did it matter that he and his beloved student had never spoken of this? They had never embraced. Perhaps, because it was never expressed, Loren's love was more potent. He viewed his love and its reciprocation in an idealized, fantasy light. He hid the expression of his love away because he knew that exposing it to the prosaic laws of reality risked exprosure of a structure that was perhaps unsound.

Never tested, he thought his love might somehow continue, and with it the possible returned love of Alex. A spell cast, but never uttered.

With Puckett the ending had been different, come much earlier. Puckett had fed on Loren's praise, growing stout and vain and increasingly conscious of his own power. His ambition, spoon-fed at first, grew stout and vain and increased the volume of his voice. Now he was going to tackle Wagner, to Loren's express disapproval. They had quarrelled about it on the trip to Portland, to their mutual surprise.

Alex, on the other hand, remained charmingly, touchingly, refreshingly free of personal vanity, and underestimated continually the ultimate worth of his voice. Loren tried to instill at least some operating measure of ambition into Alex. But Alex, in the end, sang because he liked to sing and because he sang well. It was a natural gift he had, a special grace, and he could not envision commercializing it. Alex was almost freakish in this respect. And finally it was why he left.

Loren burned to think of it, to remember himself pressuring Alex into performance, into singing on a stage, dismissing the young man's mild and completely ordinary ambitions. A stage mother without a child, that's what Loren told himself he was.

Alex hadn't shown up for his private lessons for a week before his letter came—that simple Alex letter—saying that he would not be returning for more voice lessons. He had gone to Atlanta with a friend. He had no idea what he would do there.

Amazing, Loren thought now, how much liquid is actually expelled by crying. The old sea within me. He wiped his wet face with his stout, hairy hands and then traced the contours of his head. He and James had the same prominent nose, their father's nose. A new infant chin had lately been growing, unseen, beneath his old one, and his body was stoutening. His silver hair was still shockingly thick, unlike James'.

Now he felt the corners of his eyesockets, pressed in until his vision was disturbed. Beneath that layer of flesh lay a skull, a blank blindly staring mass of bone. At some distant time his flesh would drop from his skull. He would decay. Dead. Extinct. Loren swallowed a faint moan and held the edge of the sheet up to his neck as another stream of tears began to bubble from his eyes and fall into his hair and onto the pillow. Dead, never having received his full measure of love.

Loren's big naked body, familiar with the bruising pain of his night thoughts, slowly shifted into another position.

Daniel set the breakfast table outside. He was sitting with his chin cupped in his hands, staring intently into the garden, when Loren scuffled out in his ratty old slippers. Daniel cocked his head to one side and smiled. James snapped down his newspaper and politely greeted his brother.

"Beautiful morning," Daniel said. "Have some coffee and a roll."

Neatly folding his paper, James squinted as the morning sun hit his eyes. "What will Africa be like in ten years, I wonder?"

"McDonald's," Daniel said. "Like the rest of the world."

"No one else having a sweet roll?" Loren asked, licking some sweet glaze from his fingers.

"I've had mine," James said. "And Daniel is fasting today. Once a week he doesn't eat anything, in mystical deference to the starving multitudes." His voice sounded peevish and deprecating. "He thinks it helps them, somehow."

"I've never said that it helps them," Daniel said.

"Then why do it?" James asked.

"Look, I happen to believe that we are in a position of being able to eat too much. We overeat. We overconsume everything."

"Daniel tends to harangue, as you can see," James said.

Daniel was getting annoyed. "I do not harangue," he said quietly.

"Well people don't particularly want to be overwhelmed at breakfast with your overly excited views. If you ask me, you're excited because you don't eat."

"I didn't know you took such an interest in my diet," Daniel said coolly. He turned to Loren to regain his humor. "I do harangue," he said. "But most of the time, you know, I'm very quiet. Whole weekends, sometimes, when I'm working out here in the gardens, and don't speak to a soul. But then, when I'm with people, I'm very unusual, Loren. I like to exchange views. I like to get to know people. I like to talk—talk endlessly."

"And doesn't my brother listen to you?" Loren asked. He and James looked at one another quickly, with an instantaneous sense of self-consciousness.

"When he has time he listens. Which is not to say that he hears."

"People don't listen anymore," Loren said with a heavy sigh. "Listening is becoming a lost art. People seek the distraction of sounds and noises."

Daniel leaned forward with interest. "I have an interesting theory about that," he said.

"Please spare us your theories for now," James said.

The banter up until this remark had been playful, but now it suddenly turned acidic. A curtain fell and even Loren could sense that something was wrong between James and Daniel.

Daniel was staring puzzled at James. "Why are you being so fucking rude this morning?" he said.

James was not prepared for this, and especially not in front of his elder brother. Hadn't Daniel just made their relationship unequivocably clear? James was angry and embarrassed. He sat staring intently into his coffee cup, his mind a furious blank.

Poor James! thought Loren, wishing he could somehow put his brother at ease. Turning to look surreptitiously at Daniel, he thought, Poor Daniel! James, even as a child, had always been too stern with himself. Loren had sensed instantly upon entering the house James' uneasiness. It was because Daniel was so obviously present.

Daniel, meanwhile, sat with a face set almost as hard, uncompromising and angry as James'. Pushed out of love, he thought bitterly, his eyes dry and sharp. Shoved away. James was not his enemy, but this other thing, this sour monster of self-refutation, was. Daniel had worked through this growing tension in James so often of late that he did not consider this to be a new crisis. But its intention was clearer to Daniel now. It was meant to push him away as an unresolvable embarrassment.

"I need to bathe in some dragon's blood this morning," Puckett said, standing in the terrace doors. He was wearing a white silk robe. "Have any?"

"We did, a moment ago," Daniel said. "Come and eat." His face lightened as Puckett approached the table. "You're—hey, he's wearing the carnation I gave him last night. Now here's my kind of person. Appreciates my flowers."

James turned to him. "I appreciate your flowers," he said stiffly.

Daniel was moved and put a hand on James' arm. Seeing fear, he quickly drew it back. "I hope you do," he said.

"He has the gift of immediate intimacy," Loren said, carefully weighing his words. He and James were on their way to the college, so that James could show him the grounds and his office. Puckett had remained at the house in order to go over a score.

"Who does?" James asked.

"Your friend—Daniel. He tries to make a person feel right away as if he belonged."

"In your own house?" James said.

"It's not my house."

"You own half," James insisted.

"I don't want it. It's your house, to do with as you please. I have my own house in Los Angeles and I'm perfectly content in it and don't want another one."

"The will states—"

"Fuck the will," Loren said. "Look, if you're going to be so territorial about it with Daniel and make sure that he knows it's your house—" He paused to consider, pulling on his beard. "—well, why, that's all. Relax with the goddamned house, relax with sharing it. You didn't do all that work in the garden, he did, but he doesn't claim ownership and begrudge you enjoying them. He encourages people to enjoy. I think that's good."

"He does claim a kind of ownership of them, of the gardens," James said.

This ridiculous emotional stinginess! Or had he, Loren, completely misjudged Daniel? Was Daniel really some sort of unpleasant burden on James? A usurping gigolo?

Loren looked sharply and saw the tension held in James' face, in the way he grasped the steering wheel of their parents' Mercedes as he drove, in the way he moved. Loren was himself a shambler. James was upright and precise.

"Well anyway," Loren said, "mother would be pleased to see the gardens so restored." Their mother, dead, her life over, while her sons, alive, sped along a highway, not knowing one another, strangers. It was no great feat to turn his thoughts from his deceased mother to his departed Alex. Death had many relations, some of whom were living.

"Yes," James said, "I suppose she would." The fact that the gardens were no longer derelict, with that she would no doubt be pleased. But the fact that they had been salvaged, saved, by a young man who was the lover of her younger son? What would her reaction have been, had she known?

He diverted the talk away from Daniel and the gardens and onto easier topics.

The brothers had never admitted to one another that they were gay. Both knew, or supposed in an unspoken manner, that the other knew, but details of their respective lives and loves had never been exchanged. Shyness held their tongues, and embarrassment too, producing between them an awkwardness of expression. The truth lay so very close to the surface, bulging large and obvious. Both wanted to admit it and release the unnecessary emotional disguise it entailed. This would have been much easier for Loren than for James. It would have been easier for both of them if they were closer than they were.

Their brotherhood was a problem in all of this. It would have been easier had they been strangers.

Loren simply didn't much care any longer who knew. He had reached a point in his life when all the subterfuge and camouflage, intended or not, was too bothersome and degrading to worry with. Except when it came to the men he had loved. Those two he had never told, and kept himself from telling. At any rate, his life was presenting him with far greater issues than the disclosure of homosexuality. That, in comparison, was trivial. Every man faced death, and if a man could not be what he was during the lifetime he had to be it, what good was a lifetime? A life was too easily reduced to waste, to disguise, to what-was-not rather than what-was.

Daniel, Daniel, Daniel. It didn't matter what small talk James made because Daniel was always the centrifugal force to which his thoughts returned. "Yes, I feel myself fighting against sluggishness too," he said in response to something Loren said. "All this extra work, and the research for the book, and the goddamned never-ending committees and then trying to keep up with new work. There are times when . . . God, Loren, I'm just tired. It's something beyond tired. I would like to be able to just sit and do nothing. Absolutely nothing."

"I find I've grown more relaxed in the past few years,"

Loren said. "I actually can sit—not sit and do nothing, haven't reached that state of Nirvana yet. I have to be reading, or listening to music, or doing a crossword. Walking along the beach is best for me, or going into the little sauna I've built. You can't read in a sauna. All you can do is sweat."

Through the black sheen of grief and obsession, he could still carry on perfectly normally. Loren wondered what other people went through in the deepest privacies of their minds as they dutifully went through the daily paces of life. The routines of life didn't allow for kowtowing to the secret little madnesses hiding in everyone. It was just as well.

Like many people who are extroverts because their profession requires it, Loren had friends in abundance, but not close ones. Outside of the college he preferred a kind of tempering solitude to continual socializing. After a day of heavy teaching, of numerous vocal students going through their exercises, singing their assignments, discussing various points of interpretation and vocal management; after working with his Symphonic Choir, page by page, bar by bar, sectionally and *en masse*, rehearsing new works, polishing others for performance, studying scores, reading the journals, counseling, attending musical events and departmental meetings—after hours of this every day, Loren, like James, had always been glad to retire to the relative quiet and solitude of his own home, where only the birds sang, and then always on pitch.

In his dedication to his work, Loren was very much like his brother. Unlike James, however, he did not return home to a lover, a companion. His problems and frustrations were his alone, to be faced and solved alone. Usually this suited him. He was not a lonely man, though he was inclined to be somewhat melancholic. He was like James, too, in his lack of a confiding nature.

Why then should he want suddenly to tell James what he was going through? Why did he think that might lance the

black festering depression that made his nights so saline and
sorrowful?

He wanted to say to his brother that love should never be
an embarrassment; that it was the only reality worth consider-
ing; that sour quaverings of the mind affect quality of heart.

Of course James must know all this, Loren thought. But it
was easier for Loren, the fact of his homosexuality, because
Loren did not have a real love to protect, as James did. Easier,
too, because Loren had never been, and was not now, very sexually active. The two loves of his life, Puckett and Alex, had
had an element of the erotic in them, but little in comparison to
the other reasons he found to love them.

If either Puckett or Alex had shown signs of physical affection, sexual interest, Loren would have been radiantly
happy—happier, that is, than he was simply by loving. But finally he was a little afraid that if sex entered either relationship
the quality and beauty of his love would be somehow desecrat-
ed. With a singing voice to love, with a sound that issued forth
liberated from the lungs and throat, searching, climbing, seeking perfection, love could become an issue not only of the beating heart, but of the spheres.

"The opera world must be a strange one," Daniel said as he
watered plants in the living room.

"No stranger than any other, once you get used to it,"
Puckett said, watching him.

Daniel had thrown open the windows and draperies to admit the full heft of the summer morning sun, and the riotous
shriekings of the birds. Periodically he would spot something
from the window, snatch up a pair of binoculars, run from window to window, and then scribble notes in the margins of a bird
identification book.

Puckett sat on the bench in front of the black Steinway
and half-heartedly plucked out pieces from the score of

Tannhäuser. Impossible to concentrate with the uproar of the sun and the birds and the summer day and Daniel.

A fat bee came zigzagging through the room and disappeared in a great mass of cut flowers. Sylvie, the large bedraggled dog with the hot bad breath, appeared with a large bone which she carefully laid on a rug in the sun, smiled tenderly over, eyed lovingly, and proceeded to gnaw with ferocious snappings and scrapings. A calico cat was suddenly sitting in another parallelogram of sun: Puckett saw her just as her tail was slowly curving around her paws, as though she were composing herself after being magicked into being. "Hello Edwina," Daniel said, stopping to scratch her ears as he passed. "She lives down the street," he told Puckett, "but comes over to visit."

When she saw Daniel scratching the cat, Sylvie stretched her head over to sniff Edwina, all the while carefully protecting her bone. Drawing back, she stared and then sneezed violently, agitating the dust in the sunlight. Edwina gave her a demure look, lifted a paw and began daintily to lick between her toes.

A moment later the doorbell rang. It was an older woman from a few doors down, returning a book she had borrowed from Daniel. Puckett heard them discussing a pileated woodpecker recently seen in the neighborhood.

"Busy house," Puckett said when Daniel returned.

"You probably find it all excruciatingly boring, this Saturday morning domesticity."

"No, but bewildering a little. It's something I have no time for."

"Where do you find a sense of stability in your life then?" Daniel asked. "I don't mean that housework and gardening gives everyone stability, but they do help the illusion along."

Puckett closed the score and turned around with his arms crossed. He looked at Daniel—it was something perhaps to do with those old worn jeans he was wearing, and the burnt color of his skin, the blue of his eyes, the shape of his hands. Puckett wanted to draw him close, put his tongue in Daniel's mouth, feel that body.

"I have no stability in my life," he said. "Not like you have. So long as I can sing and sign contracts I have stability of a sort. But if my voice were to go, if I suddenly decided to be lazy—down the drain it would go."

"There must be some kind of satisfaction in that, though. Taking chances," Daniel said. "At least you know that you're alive and doing what you want to be doing."

"Aren't you doing what you want to be doing?" Puckett asked.

"I seem to need certainties. I keep trying to create them, anyway."

"There's a tiresome side to both ways of life. I taught in a junior high school once, you know. On the whole I think I prefer singing."

"As far as work, I pretty much like what I do. Rare books, incunabulae, research collections—"

"Why don't you research my incunabulae?" Puckett said.

Daniel laughed. "Of course there's no stability in library work just now. But there's the romance of old books—"

"I know better kinds of romance," Puckett said.

"The smell, the feel, the type, the printing—and letters, we get collections of letters which I read through before cataloguing. Now that's a strange feeling, to be privy to such privacies. Anyway, there's plenty of intellectual romance in library work, but no stability."

"Why not?"

"Ph.D.'s, what else? The country's inundated with hundreds of cutthroat Doctors of Philosophy who would do anything to get my dear little job. Or any job, for that matter."

"You need a Ph.D. to piss nowadays," Puckett said.

"You know what I find strange? The characters I sing on stage. None of them actually work, you know."

"They foment revolution, don't they?" Daniel said. "And Siegfried works, he has to weld that sword and then go out to slay the dragon."

"He's too stupid to do anything else. And I haven't sung Siegfried yet."

"Will you?"

Puckett considered. "Some day. Yes, some day." He paused. He hit a key on the piano, hit it again and again. "But what about today?" he said in a low voice. "What about right now?"

"What about it?" Daniel said, lighting a cigarette.

"We both feel it, don't we?"

Daniel looked at him. Yes, it was mutual. It wasn't some fantasy he had concocted. They did somehow understand one another in this odd unspoken way. Sexually, at least, they were telepathic. And what, he asked himself desperately, what was wrong with that? Sheer sensual abandon—the liberation of one's body—pure feeling—pure good feeling with no guilt attached. "I'm not," he said suddenly, moving away.

"You're not what?"

"Afraid of you," Daniel said.

"Afraid of me?" Puckett let out a blast of laughter.

"I should say, afraid of myself."

"Are you?"

"Yes—no—I don't know."

"That's truthful."

Daniel went to a window. He stood looking out, running a hand through his shaggy hair. "You know, a garden is so much easier. Plants and birds and old mother earth"

"Erda," Puckett said. "I've met her. She's a bore."

Daniel smiled at him. "A garden is easier."

"Than what?"

"This," Daniel said. "This. Indoors. Now."

"This. Indoors. Now," Puckett repeated.

"The mental contortions," Daniel said. "The realization that you are doing this to me."

"I thought it was mutual," Puckett said.

"It is," Daniel said. He took a deep breath and walked over to Puckett sitting on the piano bench.

Puckett put an arm around Daniel's legs. He felt Daniel's lean, long body with slow, delicious luxuriousness. It felt ordained for his hands.

"Man, you are beautiful," Puckett said. "You know that? You are a beautiful man."

"So are you. But—look—it's just that—"

" I know what it is," Puckett said, his hand slowly moving into Daniel's shirt. He found a nipple and slowly caressed it. "It's James," he said, as he planted a first kiss on the crook of Daniel's arm. "He's your lover, isn't he?"

"Yes."

"And he wants to disguise that fact. Why?" Puckett, disguising nothing, felt Daniel's crotch, grazed it with his mouth through Daniel's jeans.

"He—no, look, it isn't right to stand here like this and talk about James. James doesn't enter in to this."

"Good," said Puckett, unbuttoning Daniel's shirt and sliding his hand in to play with the soft stomach hairs. Opening the shirt wider, he kissed Daniel's stomach, and then drew Daniel's face down to his, and covered Daniel's lips with his own.

There was a sudden loud thud in one of the windows. Daniel whirled around thinking he would see a face looking in at him with disbelieving hurt. "Jesus, what was that?" He saw in the same instant what it was. A large thrush had mistaken the clear glass of a window for unimpeded air and crashed into it. The glass was cracked. He saw the bird drop stunned into the flowerbed under the window, and rushed outside to see what he could do.

Puckett let his hand drop to the keyboard of the Steinway, and played a flat, discordant finale.

"The main idea behind this garden," Daniel said, standing with Loren on the edge of the central path, "comes from a gardening philosophy developed in England." The evening sun, late summer sun, unfurled down upon them. "Your mother must have been familiar with it. It's called paradise gardening."

"As in Garden of Paradise?" Loren asked.

Daniel nodded. "An attempt to regain Eden."

"Steal it back from God?"

"Steal it back from man," Daniel said. "It should be a place where lovers and friends can walk and feel that they're in a special place. A place for them. A place for love." He took Loren's arm in his own without thinking, felt it flinch, and instantly removed it. "Sorry, I'm in the habit of walking arm-in-arm with my friends here. I forget that people don't always like that."

"And I forget that's what friends should do," Loren said, putting an arm around Daniel's shoulder. "A place for love, you say."

"A place that accepts loving, encourages it. That's the scheme of any garden, really. They're emotional places."

"I can almost see her out here," Loren said quietly. "She always wore a straw gardening hat, and lambskin gloves."

"And she carried a basket, a trug, for the flowers she cut."

"James told you. She was a quiet and remarkable woman. She was always so happy out here. You are too, aren't you?"

Daniel smiled and nodded.

"They're your gardens," Loren said. "You're the one re-making them. I don't regard this house as mine, never did, never wanted to. It belongs to James, and you. I was never here much, you know, in the way James was. It's just never meant to me what it means to him."

"I didn't think it meant that much to him, either," Daniel said.

"Oh yes." Loren sighed as he looked around the scene of childhood. "Oh yes, it does."

"Sometimes I think James resents it," Daniel said.

"He resents anything that stirs up his emotions," said Loren. "We were not raised to be emotional, or to show emotion in any way."

"That ten year gap between you is too bad," Daniel said. "James in grade school when you're in college, that sort of thing. You know it's funny, but he's never seemed to me like a younger brother of anyone, until now. With you here he does seem like one, and it gives him another dimension. I mean, he's said things." He saw that Loren wanted to hear and went on. "For instance, that the age difference always made him feel that you were more like a parent, or an uncle; and that you were away most of the time and when you did come back, one summer, he had polio and remembers that you sat at the piano your mother bought you and played Debussy all day long."

"Played Debussy badly," added Loren.

"You wouldn't do anything but sit and play the piano."

"I remember that summer," Loren said. "It was a difficult summer for me—for James too, of course. He had polio and was having some sort of painful therapy. And I—well, I—"

"Realized you were gay?" Daniel hazarded.

Loren let out an exhalation. "Yes," he said, "that was the summer I couldn't hide from myself any more. I tried to. I played the Children's Corner Suite over and over, but I could never get it right."

"You weren't a child anymore," said Daniel.

Loren laughed. "Exactly."

"Well, being gay back then was more of a terror than it is today."

"That's true. I'm glad it's easier now," Loren said.

"For some people it's easier," Daniel said, remembering his own coming out trauma and the sudden estrangement from his family.

Loren remembered going to bed that summer with an eminent conductor who had come to give a series of master classes. Loren had been in the class. The conductor was then probably as old as Loren was now. No, not that old. How old? When was that? What year? Back when he was young, before his life was folded two-thirds away. Time and memory suddenly haunted him with a piercing sweetness. He stood now in this garden, which he had known differently as a boy; he stood in this garden, now, in his present, not an old man, but an older man. The years . . . the years . . .

"It's difficult for me to imagine James having polio," Daniel said. "He's never done more than mention it."

"Everyone was scared that he'd never walk again."

"And then my imagination fails me in one other place," said Daniel. "James as a boy. Was he ever a boy?"

Loren considered for a moment. "No, not really. Not if you mean the kind of boy who runs around in a pack and gets into mischief. He read incessantly, and he had these painstaking hobbies he'd work on with complete concentration, for hours on end. And except for one or two friends, he stayed pretty much to himself. He did have an imaginary friend when he was six or seven, I remember that."

"James did?"

"My mother thought it was amusing, but my father thought it was unhealthy. I remember him shouting at James, 'Stop playing with someone who's not there!'" They laughed

with a kind of sympathetic horror. "But try explaining to a
child that what's real to him isn't there."

"Try explaining to an adult that what's real to him isn't
there," said Daniel.

"You're right. Imagination makes kings and fools of us
all."

"Have you kept your imagination?" Daniel asked. "I
think James is afraid of his."

"To my detriment, to my everlasting shame and salvation,
yes, Daniel, I have retained my imagination. Or so I like to
believe."

Just as the light had changed quietly, imperceptibly,
from a major to a minor key, and roosted now in the highest
branches of the trees, so had Loren's mood changed from a
kind of intimate playfulness to something more sober and
reclusive. While night crept in, slowly snuffing out the light,
his mind prepared itself for the night thoughts that the light
helped to smother during the day. Death came to stand beside
him.

Daniel sensed the change. Loren stood now in a kind of
tentative, bewildered posture. Daniel wanted to touch him
again, offer the comfort of his hand. How many times had he
felt the same way towards James, wanting with a word or gesture to say that he was there, ready to listen, to understand.

"There's a streak of melancholia in the Donahue
brothers," Daniel said.

"What?" Loren roused himself. "No, not melancholic—just colic."

Around them borders of sweet alyssum glowed and
soaked the cooling air with their scent. A stand of white dahlias
hung like low exploded stars. The earth and the trees gave off a
dark, fertile exhalation.

"You're a young man," Loren said after a few moments
had passed. "And you remind me at certain moments of

someone."

"No one awful, I hope."

"Quite the contrary. I was in love with him."

"Are you still?"

"He's dead," Loren said. A small noise of indeterminate expression escaped from his throat. He felt Daniel's hand on his shoulder, and he pressed it with his own. "Dead to me, at any rate."

"I'm sorry," Daniel said.

"But you continue, you know, you continue to love someone after he's died, or you love the idea of him, or the memory. That's what's most difficult, you know, to have love without the object of your love." He looked at Daniel and smiled, then touched Daniel's face. "Don't misunderstand me," he said. "It's not because I'm a man who was in love with a man that I'm going through this emotional menopause. It's because I'm a man old enough to realize that my life is less doing now than being. It makes me wonder some times if I missed my chance."

"Maybe your chance is yet to come," Daniel suggested.

"I never used to prefer looking back to looking forward, you know, but there are times now when I don't want to look forward."

The active light had now withdrawn and the crickets were beginning to tune up with the orchestra of night. Something rattled the leaves of a close shrub. With sudden sharp notes of terror or territoriality a robin fled past, his wings buzzing. Behind them, a light went on in the house.

"And there's something else," Loren said. "I mean something to do with being a man who was in love with a man." He put his hands in his pockets and gave his baggy trousers a heft. "You see, I never told him that I loved him. It may be better that I didn't because the people we love can't always love us in return. I've always told myself that the way I love people is different somehow. Not exactly physical. But I wonder now if this difference isn't just fear. I've been afraid, even while I was in love. Afraid to do anything. Afraid to act. And it makes me sick and ashamed of myself, Daniel. I never used to be lonely. It's only after being in love that I am."

"I'm sorry," Daniel said.

Loren sniffed. "Things are reinterpreting themselves in my head. Maybe I'm like the blind man who suddenly sees. But now, goddamn it, I see and see and see and I think I'd be grateful for a little myopia. Just to rest my eyes from what seems to be the miserable clarity of it all."

"That will come, don't you think? Some kind of pause or respite will come."

"I could answer that death is the great pause, the endless respite, and isn't it better to jump in with your eyes open instead of suffering all the black suspense of waiting for the axe to drop?"

"You mean suicide?"

"I mean isn't it better to creep along and be thankful for this middle-aged vision rather than hope for blindness again? There's one thing to be said for age: you become braver. Less concerned with what people think. Stupid things lose their ridiculous importance and knowing your fear, you can fight it."

"Then you're ready to love," Daniel said. "You're finally ready."

Loren smiled at him in the darkness. "Let's go in."

They started down the path towards the lighted windows of the house.

"Thank you," Loren said on the way. Daniel shrugged his shoulders. "I mean more than that, but it just comes out as thank you."

* * * * * * *

Puckett could not get over his infatuation with Daniel. Having acknowledged it, he would not let it go. He was becoming a man who always got what he wanted, and he wanted Daniel. He had no scruples about this, no reticence. Desire brought out a fierce intention in him to possess, to overpower, overwhelm. He felt as the hound must, when it gets the first scent of fox. A wild dangerous tang was in his nose, and Puckett would do anything he could to hunt it down and make it his own.

He had been watching Daniel, and he knew that Daniel was aware of his interest. Puckett had no moral scruples about seducing another man's lover. He rather enjoyed the idea. He found James to be an annoying prig and academic snob, a man with no sensuality, no pleasure in pleasure.

Puckett's infatuation grew in this party atmosphere of raised voices and heightened spirits. Daniel had insisted on a huge spur-of-the-moment party in honor of Loren and Puckett and had then been frantic all day with preparations. A woman named Tilda came over to help him. People arrived in a continuous stream, bearing wine and food. The house was full and loud and the guests were beginning to loosen up and explore the gardens.

Daniel, wearing a Chinese jacket with a snarling Phoenix rising from embroidered flames on its back, wove in and out amongst the guests, stopping to talk and laugh. Puckett watched him with the secret pleasure of a conspirator. Daniel was intrigued by Puckett's sexual interest in him. While someone was talking, Daniel's eyes would wander away and find Puckett's. He would smile faintly and self-consciously before turning back to whomever was talking.

The people around him were Puckett's age, some few younger, some few older, but how vastly different their lives and concerns were from his. An academically liberal attitude and a commitment to some kind of general social justice seemed to prevail. They worried about the environment, about the land and the air and the sea. They seemed to believe that they could protect the world and make it a better place. And, Puckett noticed, they were all white.

A group near him was discussing political candidates and legislative issues, some sort of protective gay rights bill. How earnest, Puckett thought, how American! He realized then what a stranger he had become in his own country.

He felt a pinch and turned to see Tilda standing beside him.

"How are you?" Puckett asked.

"I love parties," she said. "This is the first time Dan's had a party here."

"Perhaps James gives the parties?" Puckett suggested.

"Are you kidding?" Tilda looked around before shaking her head. "James is definitely not the entertaining type," she said, lowering her voice.

"What? Oh no thank you, I do not smoke," Puckett said to a young man handing around a joint.

"Bad for the pipes, eh?"

"Well I do smoke," said Tilda. "Tommy give me a hit of that. This makes you sing better," she said to Puckett, holding the smoke deep in her lungs.

"I'm told that marijuana makes sex better," Puckett said.

Tilda exhaled and smiled enigmatically. "It makes you sing, my dear. Oh look, here's Dan."

Daniel was standing with two rather stiff men. "Peter, this is Francis Turner, who teaches French, and this is Dobbin Riggs."

"I've heard you sing," Francis said immediately.

"In Basel, he heard you sing in Basel," confirmed Dobbin.

"The Duke in *Rigoletto*," said Francis.

The conversation veered off into opera. Tilda poked Daniel and gave a secret nod. "Dobbin's trying to put the make on Peter," she whispered.

Daniel turned to look. It was true. He smiled at Tilda. "You know how those Dukes are," he said.

The French doors were open to the gardens and people strolled in and out talking and laughing, drinking wine or beer or lemonade. Strauss waltzes were playing. A couple was dancing happily on the terrace.

Someday, Loren thought, standing with a glass of beer and watching them, rocking almost imperceptibly back and forth in his large boatlike shoes, someday they will every one of them be dead, lying in a coffin to be buried or incinerated. From everyone at the party he snapped out life—that simple amazing possession that allowed them to walk into or out of the gardens—and returned them to rigor mortis. Those fluid joints would lock tight and the flesh—ah, that living, encasing, beautifully colored cover—would rot from their bones.

What were they all but skeletons given a few years of life? And in their cool summer frocks and thin summer shirts and shorts, a rattling assortment of femurs and tibias, fibulae and iliums, promenaded before Loren's eyes. This was the closest he could come to making light of his own morbidity. The sharp, dark, terrifying edge of his depression had been softened since talking to Daniel. As simple as an emotional outlet, Loren thought.

In the gardens, under an old apple tree, he saw two women embracing. They kissed. Their passion for one another rose. They looked into the reflective echoes of one another's eyes and kissed again. One took the hand of the other and they disappeared down a shadowy path.

A quiet, pleasurable ache rose in Loren's heart. That kind of intensely reciprocal passion would never be his. His need to love would be defused and filtered to his students, abstracted into his love of music itself. Never his the divine commonplace that made two people feel whole in one another's company.

He glanced over at his first love, Peter, laughing amongst a group of people, showing his mouthful of beautiful teeth fiercely and with intent to dazzle. He was succeeding. He created adoration around him, and that, Loren mused, was the sign of a star . . . and a potential monster. Who had unleashed this man? None other than Loren himself.

I gave him the ambition I lack, Loren thought. Too much, perhaps. Loren was convinced that Peter's voice was not ready to handle Wagner, and Wagner was the direction Peter was taking. He'd shred his voice to pieces if it meant getting to the top of his profession. And Loren had to let him do it.

Daniel came by and asked if he was enjoying himself. "In my melancholy way," Loren said.

Daniel gave Loren's beard a tug. "The party's for you, you know."

"I like seeing the house like this," Loren said. "And the gardens. Full of people. Full of life. Full of sex."

"Where?" Daniel asked.

Loren smiled towards Puckett, who had been drawn into intimate conversation with Dobbin Riggs.

"Full of himself," Daniel said. "Of course he suits himself quite well. I've never seen Dobbin Riggs cruise before. He looks like he's pretty good at it."

"And look how it fascinates old Francis Turner," Loren said.

Francis Turner was standing in conversation, his arms crossed, on the other side of the room. But he couldn't keep his eyes off Dobbin and Puckett. He didn't seem to be looking on with envy or jealousy, but rather a sharp furious fascination.

"Have you seen James?" Daniel asked.

"Not for a while, no."

"I'm going to see if I can find him."

For one overwhelming moment James thought that he was actually going to lose control, utterly lose it, and begin to shout and hurl things. Too much, too much, too much. Too much to control, too many things to do, and then all of these people, all of these people. The house of his parents, invaded, filled to the rafters with these loose, chattering friends of Daniel's: men holding hands, women with their arms around one another, examining everything in the house, inspecting the rooms, opening doors they had no right to open. News came to the house that there was nude swimming in the river. A crazy bitterness soured James' mouth, made his already tense face contract as if it were trying to keep itself from exploding.

The crest of the moment passed and the scene dropped back into a more reasonable perspective. A party, with mostly Daniel's friends, and a few of his own. He nodded to Francis Turner across the room. He had met Daniel in Turner's house. What if he hadn't gone to dinner there that night? This evening would not be happening. His relationship with Daniel was changing the very course of his existence.

He had been furious with Daniel for what seemed like months now, although it actually began with Loren's and Puckett's arrival. Alternating with this unreasonable and unreasoning gut-contracting anger was the terrible roar of love that sounded when James could see, with perfect clarity, exactly what he was doing. He was punishing Daniel. He was wronging him. Daniel had done nothing wrong. Yet James would not or could not stop himself. He was mesmerized by the force of this weird, punishing obsession. As if what he really wanted was for Daniel to give up on him, grow tired of him, and finally be driven away.

And then peace would descend, and gone would be the quick-eyed hyper-self-consciousness about appearances, about what people thought. And James was too tired to fight the rancor of the world. It required too much time and pain. It required facing a world unbearably ignorant.

"Hello, my dear," Tilda said, joining him.

"Hello," said James.

"I want to ask you something. When the hell am I going to get you to pose with Daniel in front of Vertumnus in the garden? I'll have Daniel's figure sketched in and half-painted before you even come out and model for me."

"I don't think I'm a very good model," James said.

Tilda stood directly in front of him, forcing James to look at her. "James, you are supposed to be in this painting. You're a part of it. You're part of the composition. One half-hour does not a model make. I need to play with you a little before you go on the canvas."

"I just haven't had any time to play."

"I'm painting this as much for Dan as for myself. He wants you to be in it. The two of you, out there in the gardens, will make the painting be what it's supposed to be."

"Maybe it should be something else," James said. "Just Daniel."

"I'd say this even if I weren't high," Tilda said. "You're losing him and you're a fool if you do."

A large group had gathered along the banks of the river. They lounged on the grass under the willows, sat on the bluestone stairs leading down, and swam naked in the cold, sweet water. Puckett, having extricated himself from Dobbin Riggs, idled down to this spot to be alone for a minute. He leaned against a nearby tree and watched the swimmers.

"I brought down some towels," Daniel said, appearing with a stack of them.

"Come in, come in," the swimmers called. "It's divine."

Daniel stood deliberating. "Just for a minute." He quickly shed his clothes and eased himself into the icy water with a grunt.

Puckett, seeing his chance, stripped and dove in, surfacing beside a startled Daniel.

"You've been avoiding me," Puckett said. The two of them swam away from the others.

"I've been avoiding you," Daniel admitted.

"Why?"

"You know perfectly well why," Daniel said.

Puckett swam closer, treading water beside Daniel. "I can feel your body right through the water. I can feel how hot it is."

Daniel looked quickly, nervously around. "You're making all this very difficult for me," he said.

"It shouldn't be difficult," Puckett said, "it should be easy."

"It should be, but it isn't."

"Yesterday," Puckett whispered, "if that goddamned bird hadn't crashed into the window, you would have—"

"I don't know, I don't know, yes, probably. I felt like a snake being charmed out of a basket. But now—here, in this house, no, really Peter, it's impossible."

"Come with me to Vancouver tomorrow," Puckett said impulsively.

"To Vancouver?"

"Come with me."

"I can't."

"Then come to Germany with me," Puckett said. "Come to Berlin."

Daniel stared at him, half-entranced, before diving under water. When he surfaced, Puckett said: "James doesn't understand you. I do. At least on one level I do."

"Let me be reasonable about this," Daniel said with a laugh.

"It's *not* reasonable," Puckett said. "You know that as well as I do. Perhaps you and James have something more intellectual, some mental bond, but that isn't what you and I would have. It's immediate. It's sexual."

"You don't have to keep saying that."

"Why not? Your cock knows it's true. Look, I want you. I want your body. I want you in bed with me."

"Shut up," Daniel said. "Please, shut up about it."

Puckett followed him stroke for stroke. "I'm leaving to-morrow," he said. "Flying to Vancouver and then back to Frankfurt. My time here is *up*. I sing in three weeks."

"So we'd better say goodbye," Daniel said, puffing with the exertion of the swim.

"You know I stayed here this long only because of you," Puckett said, playing his last card.

"If I went to bed with you because of pressure, it would be too quick and furtive. We wouldn't enjoy it and damn it, Peter, I know it would be enjoyable. That's the problem. But I couldn't do anything with James here, and I'd rather say no than have it be a nothing."

"It wouldn't be," Puckett said. "Look, I'm dying for you. No man's ever made me feel so hot."

"Unfortunately I tend to form attachments," Daniel said. "The modern world frowns on this, I know, but there you are."

"You are romantic."

"Horribly fucking romantic," Daniel laughed, climbing out of the water. He grabbed a towel and began to rub his shivering flesh.

"Come to me in Berlin," Peter said, beside him. Before Daniel could answer, Puckett put a finger on his lips. "Don't say yes or no. Just think about it. And remember that I want you there."

Daniel hurried into his clothes.

"Is your Phoenix symbolic, Danny?" someone asked of his jacket.

"Everything is symbolic of something," Daniel said, and quickly made his way back to the house.

Yet another group had gathered around the table in the dining room. James saw a drop of wine fall onto the table and envisioned it forever marring the surface his mother had always kept polished to mirror-like perfection. When no one was looking, he surreptitiously wiped away the spot of wine.

He thought of his study, his work, with a kind of longing: away, away, alone and in control. The solid pleasure of facts. Instead of having to make small talk.

Earlier he had seen Daniel talking briefly with Loren. He had seen Daniel touch Loren's arm and tweak Loren's beard, and the sight had infuriated James. It didn't matter in the least that Loren looked amused and relaxed. James saw this as an electrifying affront, and intolerable effrontery. His mind had been churning ever since, figuring out ways to use this against Daniel. Since Tilda's comment, his emotions were dancing in a *Walpurgisnacht* and he gave himself up to the bleak, bitter glory of them.

When he saw Daniel, his hair wet, a towel in his hand, enter the kitchen, James quickly followed him. He closed the door behind him so they would be alone. Daniel, glancing around his shoulder, smiled and began to decant some wine. "I went for a quick swim," he said.

The last of the summer sun flowed past the kitchen windows and searched with red-hot gold through the flowerbeds, pinned itself to trees, preened in the mirrors of waxy leaves.

Daniel spilled some wine and swore. "Shit—I'm so nervous tonight."

"I came in here to ask you something," James said. "To talk to you."

"What about? Here, help me with this, will you? I'll take these and you take those."

"Can I say what I want to say?"

Daniel put down the tray he was holding. "What is it?"

"I wanted to say that—" James looked at his shoes and

tapped the stem of his pipe against the kitchen counter. He thought, I should not say any of this. "It's Loren."

"What about him?" Daniel asked.

"I don't think you should touch him as I've seen you doing."

Daniel felt his face hardening. He said nothing.

"I think it embarrasses him," James said.

"No, what you mean is that it embarrasses you." Daniel tried to calm himself and hold back his anger by repeating the incantation with which he had lately forgiven James so much: he's overworked, overworked, tense, tense, he does love you, love you . . .

"Yes," James said. "You know perfectly well that I've never—" he lowered his voice, "—told him."

"Told him what?"

"That we're lovers."

"Are we?" Daniel said. He took a deep breath and shook his head. "James, I don't know what to do anymore with these ridiculous things you say. I shouldn't have to defend or vindicate my actions, or apologize for them. They're my actions, and I stand by them. But you know—no, I really do not know whether to be angry or to cry."

"Don't be the first and don't do the second."

"First of all this crap about where I was going to sleep. I gave in and let you humiliate us by giving in. Then all that stuff yesterday at breakfast, trying to shut me up, trying to embarrass me. And now this."

"I'm sorry," James said crossly. "That's the way I am."

"What happened to the man who climbed a tree and asked me to come away with him?"

"What happened to the Daniel who said he understood me and would be discreet?"

"This has nothing to do with discretion!" Daniel said. "This is our house, and these people are our friends."

"Your friends," James said.

"Yours, too, if you'd let them be." He turned away, his face dark and confused. "Have people really proven themselves to be so tiny and mean that they've warped you this way?"

"Warped?" James said, insulted.

"Yes, warped. When something like affection is seen as so bloody dangerous that you have to make me continually self-conscious about it, here where we live . . . I'm not damning you by saying that, and I'm not for Christ's sake saying that being gay has warped you, but the fact that it's never let you relax for one second with who you are . . . *shit*," he spat, too angry and emotional to finish.

"Confused semantics," James said with a brittle voice. "If, as you say, I've never relaxed with who I am, and that is because a part of me is gay, it follows that my being gay is an integral part of what's warped me."

Daniel stared at him disbelievingly. "Don't shut me out with the weird logic of your wordplay," he said. "My mind isn't as precise as yours is. It doesn't know how to torture me because I never taught it to. You know fucking well what I was trying to say."

"I don't, please tell me."

Daniel held his breath for a moment before speaking. "Being gay doesn't make you or anyone warped, but being gay and not being able to be gay—not being able to show affection when you want to, and having to hide such a big part of your life—"

"It's not a big part of my life," James said.

"Then I'm not!" Daniel cried. "Christ, you are as lazy as you were when I first met you."

James thought of all his endless worrying over work and could only exclaim, more in surprise than anger, "Lazy?"

"Lazy towards yourself," Daniel said quickly, trying to

force his words in before James' mind snapped shut in self-de-
fense. "Lazy towards you. What good does all your work do
you, what fucking good I'd like to know, if when you stop
working you don't want to be who you are? Or don't know who
you are? That's the lazy I'm talking about. You can't be the
untenured professor and scholar all the time because I'm here
to confound that if nothing else does. I love you, even though
you make me not even know what that means anymore. It's
useless," he muttered, turning away again. "You know, I'm
not going to say another word. I am fucking tired of having you
fight me. I see nothing but barbed wire in your head."

He picked up the tray of glasses and just as quickly put it
down again. "I will touch your brother if I feel like it because
he's a grown man and he can tell me if he doesn't like it. But
he does like it. You may not want to believe that, but it's true.
Your brother is gay. He's told me. And I'm telling you,
James, that you are absolutely no different from the imaginary
people you think would be disgusted by your sexuality. You
are those people. You are disgusted with yourself and your emotions and I won't excuse you any more. You are an incomplete
man—unfinished—denying everything that's possibly sane
and good in order to believe in all the shit. You have no perspective. You are haunted. You believe in what you know to be
wrong for yourself. Your life is a nightmare."

James glanced quickly at Daniel, saw how his face had
darkened, set itself. Not Daniel's face at all. A blank void-like
darkness was rising in the room, slowly and quietly sucking out
colors, erasing the dumb life of things seen. And outside, a
dark sudden shape cut past the window, followed by a sharp,
hollow, frightening cry. A bird, a bird, James said to himself.
But it might have been a part of himself.

"A person doesn't ch-ch-change so suddenly," James
stuttered. Embarrassed, he looked away. It had been years
since he stuttered; and as he did so, a new thought presented

itself for inspection. I am jealous of Loren. James' sudden humiliation could go no further than this.

Daniel, hearing him stutter, seeing his panic, immediately reached over and took James' arm. James drew away. "A person doesn't change so suddenly," James said, shutting his eyes with relief when his words flowed unimpeded.

"Maybe never," Daniel said. "But that's something I've never wanted to believe. That would make the world too dark for me."

The moves of love; the fragile, difficult moves. Daniel stepped behind James and put a hand on his tensed shoulder. The kitchen door swung open and Tilda, a high rush of laughter and conversation sweeping in with her, entered with an empty pitcher filled with lemon rinds.

"Oh—I was just going to help—"

Neither James nor Daniel moved. They stood as if they were being photographed one last time, James with his hands flat on the counter, head bowed, Daniel behind him with his hand on James' shoulder.

"I'm just coming," Daniel said, his voice dull. He moved away from James, all the while looking at him, picked up the tray and brushed past Tilda.

October

1972

J ames asked for any final comments and then adjourned the meeting. Chairs honked on the tiled floor as people stood gathering their notes and papers, stubbed out cigarettes and drained the tepid dregs of coffee from styrofoam cups. The committee members brushed at their clothes, retrieved their coats, fell to talking again in small groups. The room was insufferably hot and James was sweating and light-headed when he stood.

"I think the recommendation as it stands is not clear enough—"

"That's not what I object to, what I object to is—"

"We should send it back to the curriculum committee first and then sée what—"

"*Their* recommendation was completely unacceptable as far as I'm concerned—"

There were a finite number of words which a person learned after a year or so of committees, and these could be rearranged in various phrases to express anything. Committee language. Shuffling things back and forth from one tired group to another, recommending, compromising. James was sick of it all in this hot stuffy room, tired. He slipped away before any-one could corner him with more of it.

"James!" The voice rang down the hallway and he turned to see Martha Johanneson, a new colleague in history, trotting after him. "I have something for you," she said, smiling with anticipation as she opened her bag. "This is your Halloween treat." She handed James a large marshmallow pumpkin wrapped in cellophane. "You deserve it for chairing that com-mittee."

Please, James prayed, please don't think I'm an avail-able bachelor. Please don't ask me over for a drink. "Thanks," he said. "I'd forgotten it's Halloween. Or does this really mean that I'm a pumpkinhead?"

Martha was thirtyish and casually brilliant. She had writ-ten her controversial doctoral thesis on "The Role of Women in the Slave Trade." Tall, slender, good-humored, her loose blond bob of hair was forever flying about her face as she dashed from one thing to the next. Her large green eyes never flinched behind her large round glasses, giving her a strangely appealing owlish appearance.

"Can I buy you a drink after that?" she asked, jerking her head in the direction of the conference room. Her hair chimed and rocked back into place. They started down the hallway. "Or better yet, come over to my place and have one."

"I think I'll decline this time, Martha," James said, and yet he didn't want to. Looking out, he saw the dark soaked Oregon sky, the horsechestnut trees on the campus grounds tossing in the wind and throwing off large wet brown leaves, and he thought of the empty house. He wanted companion-ship that night, a fire, talk and music, a late Beethoven quartet and brandy. He decided he would accept if Martha pressed him.

"All righty," she said. "Some other time."

James wavered for a moment, watching the trees swaying

in a strong wind which couldn't be heard through the glass—odd, like watching a movie without sound.

"I've got some preparation to do for tomorrow," he said.

"Tomorrow and tomorrow and tomorrow," said Martha. "When does an academic have time for what they call a private life?"

"During the summer. Unless you're a fool, like me, and teach in summer session and do research for a book as well." Summer. Such a potent word. Summer, summer. Hot sunny days, swimming in the river with . . . his mind gulped down the name . . . Daniel. Walking through the garden. Not that he'd had much time for those pleasures. Now that they were over, he exaggerated them.

They walked silently on, the rubber soles of Martha's shoes squeaking comically. Outside, the rain lanced down, pitting against the windows, and the trees blew and blew in the wind. A loud shriek of combined laughters rose behind them from the conference room, followed by a babble of loud, excited voices.

James and Martha reached the double glass doors and stood buttoning their coats, preparing to meet the autumn weather. I can't bear that gray sky, thought James; for another four months I'll have to live with skies like that. He felt that he had missed all the sun, the sun he exaggerated so.

"Do you like living alone in that big old house?" Martha asked. They each pushed a door and stepped out into a cold, rain-pierced wind. "Aren't you lonely there by yourself?"

"Not really," James said. "Why didn't I bring an umbrella today? Good night, Martha, thanks for the pumpkin." He hurried down the walk to his Mercedes, holding the collar of his coat tight around his throat.

But he was lonely, there was no getting around it. The old pattern of his life, pre-Daniel, could not be resumed as easily as he thought. He could do the same things, make out the same timetable for himself, but it all lacked weight, a certain substance and, well, meaning.

He regulated his days with empty formulae. Time no longer slipped fast away, it stalled and had to be pushed. Leaden hours, alone, pacing through the large quiet house, thinking there was something more he had to do but not finding it. Daniel must have absorbed some of the hours from his day just by living with him. There had never been enough time then. Sometimes James had actually regarded Daniel as "a thing to do."

Foolish, this thinking back, foolish and worthless. But he couldn't help it. It was his way of tormenting himself and accepting the guilt squarely, on his own shoulders. He had thought—he must have thought, though it seemed unlikely and unlike him—that he was somehow immune, protected.

He had sometimes thought that things would be so much easier without the burden of loving that Daniel placed on him. But never had he really expected that Daniel would finally put together all the not-meant-really words and gestures and see the thing completely. See that James no longer wanted him. Because that wasn't true, and never had been.

Yet there it was, clear enough when Daniel spelled it all out. And then James burned, damning the propulsion of all those half-conscious desires to drive Daniel away from him. He wouldn't wait to have Fortuna and her wheel do it. He would do it himself. He would fulfill the prophecy he had lain on himself years earlier: he might love another man, but it would never last, and the other man would leave.

How reckless we become when we have near us a person who inspires both our best and our worst fantasies. What stupidity, he thought now, to play with love, tinker with it, take it apart and reassemble it to suit momentary fancies. Cheap, he had held love—very cheap.

Now that Daniel had gone, James regarded their separation as final. It never occurred to him that he could follow Daniel and try to win him back. He had too little faith in himself to try. What if he did try again and failed? Then he would have to suffer over again what he had already suffered. He would have to mash down hope another time.

And, after all, they were not movie stars playing in a film, with infinite time and resources on their hands, with money and predictable plot-fitting romantic emotions. He had to work. To get away, Daniel had taken a leave of absence, risking coming back to find his job taken over by a Ph.D. James was in the middle of the term, and could not do such a thing. It would be thoroughly unprofessional. There were times when emotions simply had to be stalled or allowed to disintegrate.

A job lasted longer than a love, and one often gave more to it.

The doorbell rang and outside, huddled under an umbrella, were the first of the trick-or-treaters. They fumbled with their bags, faces turned up and waiting to see what they would be getting. How greedily calculating children had become! James thought. Some didn't even bother to say the formula, "Trick or treat!", but merely stood with their bags open, ready for a deposit and then to dash away to the next house.

James self-consciously plunked beautiful red apples into their bags. When one boy whined in an irritating voice, "Ick, apples! Ain't you got any candy bars?" James ignored his bag and shut the door without giving him anything.

Obviously it would be impossible to work uninterruptedly while this was going on. He wished now that he had accepted Martha's offer and could be with an adult rather than having to face these youthful victims of tooth decay. He poured himself a brandy and put on some music. Outside, the wind throttled the mountain ash tree, hissing through its small brown leaves, and rose to a moan as it cut past a corner of the house. And the memory came back like a habit, came with the sound of the wind, and he heard Daniel saying, "Listen, listen to the wind. It's the most ancient of sounds."

The next group was tiny, almost pathetic, little more than toddlers. They looked completely bewildered as they stared up with faces bright with fright, lipstick, rouge and paint. "What do you say?" prompted a mother standing behind them. "Trick-treat!" the children chimed mechanically.

"What are you?" James asked one child, dropping an apple into her bag.

The child stared at him with wide, terrified eyes and finally whispered, "Don't know," before darting back to her mother.

"Merry Christmas," James said absently as they toddled off, tripping over their costumes, the mother shouting instructions. They were herded into a sinister black car of enormous proportions and whisked off.

James closed the door and looked up, startled, as he entered the house. For a moment it had shifted its visual emotion. It stared at him blankly, unacceptingly, pushing him back rather than coaxing him to enter. The giant ferns were beginning to look uncomfortable, and he could trace his initials in the dust that had accumulated on the *ficus*; spiders hung and spun traceries in the jade plant and Norfolk pine and the palms. James hadn't the time to spray them and it seemed rather absurd to ask the cleaning woman to dust the plants. But there they were now looking at him with disgust for his neglect.

Tilda's unfinished painting stood in the hallway, waiting for her to pick it up. James hated to look at it but forced himself to do so. There was Vertumnus, in the center of the garden at high noon. The sun fell evenly into the picture, giving a primitive, unearthly irradiation to the greens of grass and leaves. Daniel stood to one side of the pagan god, slim, naked, the weight of his body casually resting on a spade. Beside him, where James should have been, there was a blank area where the canvas had been primed but not painted.

When the doorbell rang again it was two costumed teenagers. They greeted James enthusiastically.

"Aren't you guys getting a little old for trick and treating?" James asked as he gave them each an apple.

"Too old? Like what difference does it make how old you are?" said one.

"It's a trip, man," said the other, who was dressed in a dramatically beautiful but unidentifiable costume. "Like, just putting on a costume and like walking down the street and like no one minding—it's far-out."

"Like, it's the one night you can do it and people like, like it."

"We give the junk to our sibs—it's just nice to feel people, like, you know, generous."

"You should try it, man, bet you'd enjoy it. Thanks for the apple."

Capes billowing in the wind, the two hooded Halloweeners walked off into the night. The leaves of the mountain ash hissed and a bough creaked. It was no longer raining, and pale silver cloud continents migrated through the dark windy skies. The air smelled wet, fresh and somehow lonely.

Suddenly heavy with emotion, James walked back into the living room, turning back automatically when the doorbell rang once more. For a moment he was sorely tempted to ignore it. The sight of another gaggle of greedy children was not something he wanted to see. But the thought of the last two teenagers changed his mind. The one night when people—even if it was in the wrong way—were expected to be generous. He opened the door, trying to smile.

No one was waiting. No little disguised faces looked up to him. The wind, reminding, sizzled through the leaves and shook the shrubs in the front of the house. Jokers. Pranksters.

He stepped back and was about to go in again when something lifted and dropped near his feet. Pushed by the wind, it went softly scraping off down the front walk. Litter dropped by a trick-or-treater, James thought, going out to retrieve it.

He picked it up and looked at it in the light of the coronaed moon. He shivered. A mask. No dimestore fairy princess or pirate, although it was as light and easily ruinable as any modern mask. It was the face of a man. From what James could see, it was the face of a perfectly ordinary man.

November

1972

Puckett stood in front of a large brightly-lit mirror staring at his open mouth as he sang vocal exercises. Up went his voice, up again, higher, higher. The star on top of the tree was a bright full high C, after which the exercises reversed themselves and the voice came tripping down, lower, lower, to the darkest part of his range.

"Two octaves, that's what I've got!" Puckett said delightedly. It was obvious that he loved listening to himself sing as much as having others hear him.

He came swashbuckling out of the bathroom, wielding an imaginary sword, threw it aside and took Daniel by the shoulders, singing what Tannhäuser sings when he pleads with Venus for his freedom: "*O Königin! Göttin! Lass mir ziehn!*"

"Wrong sex," Daniel said.

"I wish I'd sounded this good for Frau Vogelkind-Schneiderhasten yesterday," Puckett said. The good Frau, a German opera star in the Forties and Fifties, was Puckett's revered teacher. "She came all the way from Munich to hear my Tannhäuser and hobnob with her old cronies at the opera house, but I wasn't up like I am tonight. *Mensch*, am I up tonight!" He danced around the room in fencing position. "There was a *wunderschon* fencing instructor at the house yesterday and I arranged for some sessions with him while I'm here. A young guy—Hungarian, I think—and with such a sweet little ass poured into his leotards."

"An opera house must be a strange place," Daniel said.

"I love it! I adore it! I love this house—my voice sounds so good in it!"

"It certainly sounded good opening night."

"Oh, a couple of rough spots—nerves," Puckett said. He loved to be reminded of opening night, his first *Tannhäuser*. He was still floating from the success of it.

The reviews, although each had mentioned his skin color (*"der junge schwarze Heldentenor aus Amerika"*; "the young black Heldentenor from America" he was invariably called), were nearly unanimous in their praise for his singing. True, one critic said that he was still rather clumsy on stage, but another made up for it by describing his characterization of the sinner-knight as "passionate, with all the brash, stumbling ardor of youth." His voice reminded one writer of Melchior, another of Bjoerling, still another of Windgassen, yet each found some unique quality in it as well. Was this his blackness? They were fascinated. Peter Puckett had become known in Berlin.

"La donna é mobile," he sang, and advanced towards Daniel, bumping and grinding.

Yes, he'd been offered more roles in Berlin the following year, and though he had already taken on as many engagements as he felt he could without straining his voice, he had told his agent to fit in whenever possible what Berlin offered. And *ja*, he would sing the role twice more next spring to fill in for the star tenor who had to cancel early due to contractual difficulties, even though it would mean flying in from an engagement in Koblenz on a Thursday night and singing again on Friday. So long as he knew this far in advance, he could give less in the Koblenz performance in order to save himself for Berlin the next night.

Koblenz! He had been awed, positively thrilled when they first hired him, five years earlier. In such places one learned the basics, built one's repertoire. Now, of course, he'd fulfill his obligations and then shake off the smaller provincial houses. They expected it. It was a process of moving up—if you could—and on. Already Hamburg was interested in a *Rigoletto*, and, of course, an *Otello*. At last they'd have a real Moor for their money.

"Aren't you going to tire yourself?" Daniel asked. "You do have to sing tonight."

Puckett was immediately sober. "Yes, I should be taking it easy. I do get frantic, though, every time I think of being trapped in Venusberg with my darling Swedish Ingeborg. I have to touch all that fat, you know. Nice kid, but I'd hate to be really trapped in the Cave of Love with her."

"She's not that fat," Daniel said. He had met her opening night, backstage. There was a big pimple on the end of her nose. "And anyway, with a voice that good—"

"It turns steely, it's a monotonous voice," Puckett said. "She's afraid to do anything but sing the notes—small wonder Tannhäuser wants to get away."

"You know you really could be more generous to people," Daniel said, annoyed. He was sickened by this side of Puckett, the side that dismissed others in his profession with such nasty exaggeration. He didn't know that every singer in the world at this point of his career was still Puckett's rival on stage, nor did he know what subtle and not so subtle humiliations Puckett had, in the past, been made to endure because of his race.

Puckett hunched his shoulders, smiled foolishly the smile of one who is trying to feel ashamed, and crept over to the bed where Daniel lay. "I'm sorry. *Es tut mir leid,*" he said, stretching out beside him, not embracing so much as imprisoning Daniel in his arms.

"Who isn't your enemy?" Daniel asked.

"You're not," Puckett said, still holding him. "Baby, baby," he whispered, rocking Daniel, kissing his ears, his neck.

"You seem to hate everyone—no one's left but you."

"All right, all right, I said I was sorry," Puckett said impatiently. "Don't make a big scene out of it, I get enough of those on stage."

"Yes, okay, okay." Daniel was silent for a moment. "But really, you know, after this—what?"

"After what what?"

"After Berlin what?"

Puckett rolled onto his back and covered his eyes with his arm. "After Berlin I return to Koblenz and Essen and all those provincial houses in the *Ruhrgebiet*. At least there's Cologne coming up."

"I meant—us."

"Have you decided?"

Daniel got out of bed and stretched. "No. But I want to go somewhere without people, I think. Somewhere without industry. Where I can just walk and think until my money runs out."

"You know why I'm not asking you to go back with me, don't you?" Puckett asked.

Daniel sat on the edge of the bed and put a hand on Puckett's massive chest. The tough, springy hair formed a perfect V. "I never expected that. Really, Peter, I didn't."

"There's something in you that latches onto people, and goes deeper than it ever could with me. I'm not like that."

"I know."

"I need many people. You want one. We have different constitutions."

Daniel spoke in Puckett's ear. "You let me come to you when I needed to come to someone. I didn't want to be alone at first, but I do now." He stroked Puckett's belly.

"You do understand?" Puckett uncovered one eye. Daniel nodded. "Because it's strange, but I do worry about you."

"How awful. And I worry about you."

Puckett was interested and sat up. "How is that?"

"You'd only be pissed if I told you." Daniel got up again and paced restlessly to the windows overlooking a section of the *Grünewald*. "This cold northern light," he said, looking out at the flat, gray, unwelcoming Berlin sky. The light was hard, alien, pressing down on the tops of the startled, frozen pines. "It's getting to me." He pressed his hand against the glass. "That's it of course."

"What's it?"

"The light. It's so different from the light in my garden. What *was* my garden."

"You think more about those fucking gardens than about James," Puckett said.

"When I think of one I'm thinking of the other." He turned to Puckett. "That hasn't interfered, has it? I mean in the sexual side of this, between us?"

"What other side is there?"

"Has it interfered?" Daniel asked again.

"No," Puckett said, holding out a hand. "I knew it would be good. We both did. I love your body. I love you in bed. Just don't fall *in love* with me, *Schatz*, whatever you do."

"Wouldn't dream of it," Daniel said drily. Puckett was moving up, and he wanted no checks or hindrances as he climbed. But love was, for Daniel, a challenge, a dare to accept into your life something that must change it. For some people, for people like James, love had to remain a timid thing, reticent to expose itself; it had to sit with a red embarrassed face, a thick tongue and twitching feet, like a child given beautiful new shoes and told that dancing or walking would damage them. Love could never survive when it was forced to deny itself. And if love was a challenge, then James had refused to fight for its life and honor.

Daniel thought of that last talk, in the kitchen, the horrible flatness he had felt within himself when he knew James would do nothing. The simplest statement from James, even then, could have made Daniel change his mind. But no, he didn't want to go over those last days again, those terrible winding-up days.

And could he love Puckett? No. The past three weeks had been an odd assortment of conflicting emotions, but out of them all came the certain knowledge that he would never fall in love with Puckett. Nor Puckett with him. There was no sorrow in this, no guilt, only a kind of bewilderment.

Excitement surrounded Puckett now and Daniel could not keep up with it. He could not keep up with or find much interest in the groups of people surrounding Puckett at parties and social events. It was when he and Puckett were in such crowds that Daniel wondered why he had come to Berlin and why he stayed on. He had to dart into dark corners simply to be by himself and catch his breath. Grief was pounding at the door, but in this odd theatrical atmosphere a real emotion seemed completely out of place. Did these people feel? Of course they did, but the idea was to pretend that they didn't.

Daniel was afraid to face the grief he knew was waiting for him. He had felt too much of it in the past to welcome it again. Once or twice, when he was alone, he had opened the door—but seeing the enormity of what was waiting for him, he slammed it shut again. Now it could no longer be kept out. His life had changed and he must accept it.

He tended to brood slowly over great hurts, and he had wanted to ease himself into this new period of change and sadness. Enough time had by now elapsed to make his ending with James seem more real than it had at first, and now that he and Puckett would soon be leaving one another, he almost looked forward to solitude.

Better to feel things, even pain, he thought, than hysterically to avoid them. He had not stopped loving James, and he would have to endure the metamorphosis of that love from an active to a passively inert part of his life. Something once living would have to be helped to die. That was the pain, that was what waited.

"Peter, is romance to you something that's only on stage?" he asked. "A kind of operatic cliché that you have to keep repeating over and over again until it doesn't mean anything?"

"As far as I'm concerned, romance is nothing but glorified sex," Puckett said. "And I'd rather have the glorified sex without the expectation of romance. It's a cliché because people are too aware of it and want it too badly. It's a cliché because they know just what it's supposed to be."

"And by expecting or forcing it, it becomes a kind of selfish fantasy?"

"Yes, just that," Puckett said.

"Gruesome, the ways we're made so self-conscious of ourselves."

"Why gruesome? I'd just as soon have the nonsense pared away because I don't have time for it. I don't want its clutter and crying in my life. I want my consciousness, *Mensch*, because my consciousness makes my life exactly what I want it to be."

Daniel eased himself into a chair, holding his stomach and staring at his toes. "Gruesome, I mean, because it does make us all so false, so different from what we could be. And gruesome because there's this part of me that's never satisfied except by things that have more to do with *not* being conscious of them. Just being a part of them. Just being connected, without the burden of analyzing. That's what I wanted him to be, and that's what I wanted the gardens to express."

He leapt up to confuse the rush of tears that suddenly wanted to fall. But where to move, where to go? He was so ac-

customed to opening the terrace doors and being able to step
out into the grace of the gardens.

Puckett undid his robe, lifted his arms, and beckoned to
Daniel. Daniel went to him. Such dumb comfort in a pair of
arms that held you, rocked you, touched your hair. Puckett's
warm skin, the wiry bristle on his chest. There was a kind of
forgetting in sex, in recitals of the body alone.

"It hasn't been a bad semester so far," Loren said, giving little
tugs to his beard.

He and James sat drinking Irish coffees, a fragrant pine
fire snapping and chattering in the fireplace. The wind rose for
a moment, rain splashed noisily on the windows.

"The rewards of teaching," James said, standing by the
mantel, looking down into the fire. "A good semester for me is
when I get one or two students who want to learn, who are willing to learn. At times I think it's only for that one or two that I
stay in teaching."

Loren shifted in his chair. "Learning," he said, and then
in a sudden rush, too impatient to put it off any longer, "You
must know or have some idea why I came up to see you in the
middle of a semester. As usual it's difficult for us to come out
with it." Loren looked at the trim, middle-aged man by the fire,
his brother, a person with a shared history and a private one.
The distances between them—why hadn't he worked harder to
break them down?

"Daniel," James said.

"And us—you and I too, finally."

James drained his drink. The thick combination of Irish
whiskey, coffee and cream warmed his stomach. He fidgeted,
decided to sit, decided to stand, jabbed the logs with the poker
until they popped and spit. "Yes."

Loren twined some hairs around his fingers. "In the first

place, we're both gay. Isn't it about time we said that to one another?"

James nodded, searched for his pipe, found it, filled it.

"We can't talk about Daniel if we don't come out with this. Christ, haven't we both known for ages and refused to face it with one another?"

"I never knew until now, hearing you tell me," James said, tamping tobacco. "I may have *thought* so before, or wondered, and even been told by Daniel—because you told him. But I never *knew* because it's unfair and frankly dangerous for a person to think he knows something like that about another person."

" 'Something like that,' " Loren said.

"I could have built up a whole life around you on the supposition that you were homosexual, but I've spent most of my adult years being afraid of those sorts of labels. I know the harm they can do."

"So do I," Loren said. "So do I."

"I regard everything as rumor and idle gossip until it's unequivocally verified by the person in question—if he wishes to verify it. One of the rules I live by," James said, striking a match and sucking the flame into the bowl of his pipe.

"But now you know."

"Now I know," said James, tossing his match into the fire. "And of course I do not deny it myself, though one could conceivably argue that without sex, one is not homosexual. Without—" He made a vague gesture.

"Without Daniel," Loren said. James looked surprised. "I would argue just the opposite," Loren said, "that one remains gay even without sex."

James laughed once, perfunctorily, and waved away the cloud of smoke hovering around his head. "I'm glad anyway that we've cleared the air," he said awkwardly.

What had Loren expected? Wild embraces, exclamations of joy and relief, comparison of notes, a pledge of new brotherhood? Certainly not this frigid reserve. "Daniel told you about our talk in the garden then?"

"Only that you had told him that, about yourself. We had an argument that night. I—" He stopped, sensing how eager he was to tell this to someone. "I thought you might have been uncomfortable with that crowd of his friends, and he himself being so—lavish—and indiscriminate in his—physical affections. In the way he handles himself."

"I appreciated it. I wish I could be more like that myself. It's habit not to be."

"Yes, well I didn't know that, did I? You hadn't told me, so I didn't know."

James, obviously, had been hurt that he was not first confided in. But that, Loren told himself, would have been quite impossible, for then, as now, James had been strained and tense and not an obvious choice for anyone's confidences.

"I wanted to tell you," Loren said. "I've always wanted to tell you. But we've had this wall between us. We haven't been close."

"Yes, I'm aware of that. At any rate, not to belabor the point, I asked Daniel to stop—and because he was angry and hurt, he told me about that, about you."

"You asked him to stop what?"

"To stop touching you," James said, a staccato-like precision to each word.

Loren pulled at his beard, ran his large hands through his unmanageable hair. "My God—were you jealous then?"

"I may have been, though not excessively."

"I'm . . . sorry for that," Loren said. "I find Daniel a very potent, a very attractive person. And he, I think, found me—well, never mind, I don't know what he found me. But none of this was sexual. It was that he was receptive towards

me at a time when I especially needed it. He is one of those
people you can look at and think, he will understand."

"And did he?" James asked. "Understand? He's very
good at that."

"I'm more grateful than he'd ever believe. It wasn't that
he did anything directly. But just by listening one night, by
understanding, or saying he understood, he helped to break
down something black and heavy in my mind. In my heart. I
needed to tell things, needed someone to listen, and he
listened. Sort of a confession."

"We should begin canonization proceedings at once,"
James said tersely.

Triple jealousy, Loren thought sadly. Poor James. Jealous that he had not been told first that Loren was gay, jealous of
Loren himself, and now—so it sounded—jealous of Daniel's
ability to be close to people.

"No miracles were performed," he said, trying to lighten
the conversation. "I wasn't completely cured, I'm still not,
but I'm a hell of a lot better than I was when I came here last
summer. And I do think of that talk with him out in the gardens
as a kind of signpost, a turning in the road."

"You have to fight with devils?" James asked, an amazed
puff of smoke rising form his pipe. "You?"

"All of my life, for Christ's sake. Didn't you think I had
any?"

James' curiosity was intense. What could someone like
Loren suffer? "What was it, the devil, this last time?"

Loren shifted in his chair. "A great sense of my mortality.
Feeling suddenly small and self-conscious about . . . just being alive. Being afraid of death, or rather unable to accept it as
a part of my life, and yet being fixated on it. And thinking that
maybe I'd done the wrong thing at one point or another in my
life, not said something I should've said. All the black terrors
we have to live through in order to be alive, I suppose."

"And has being homosexual been one of those black terrors for you?" James asked. "Has it been a demon?"

"Once it was. I suppose it is for everyone when they first come out. Who the hell knows what to do with it? Where can you go just to talk to somebody about it? There's no place to go and hear someone say, It's all right. Because it is all right. It's not tragic. Even if it's taken me almost fifty years of my life to come around to being able to say that."

"Well it is, it is with me," James said. "It has been a black terror and a demon. I haven't changed, I doubt that I can after living so long with an attitude about myself. I won't change," he said grimly. "I can't see the necessity now. When I'm by myself it doesn't matter."

"Oh, but it does, it does," Loren said, rubbing his knees. "You're still gay, even if you're by yourself."

"That's what was so splendid and awful about him," James said, suddenly drenched with emotion. "This blindness he insisted on having. It was so imcomprehensible to me. He'd say that if you weren't able to be unconscious of yourself when you loved, then you had to work at it until you were, until you felt . . . just as good and natural as anyone in love should feel. He was always wanting to help me to change—to become that way—unconscious of love. But I can't be, I couldn't. With him perhaps it was natural, but that only made it more difficult for me. I always have been, and I suppose I always will be." He stopped, his hands trembling, and puffed, trying to block the frustration of remembering, of feeling, of seeing things more clearly now that Daniel was gone. I'm like all cowards, he thought: braver when the danger is past.

"Why would that have made it more difficult for you?" Loren asked.

"Because it wasn't natural in me—that feeling! Being in love."

"Don't be a fool. Of course it's natural. What's unnatural is denying it. Being forced to deny it. Men are still embarrassed to love men."

"I was in love," James said, nodding once, assuring himself. "But in my own way, and that was only half-good enough for him. And he couldn't understand why, he could never understand *why*."

"And we do?"

"Of course we do! Our professions, our generation, all that we've been through in our lives or known we could go through if we weren't careful. Our own little chunk of unrecorded psycho-history. We've had to keep ourselves in the shadows if we wanted to get ahead. Even I know that."

Loren was silent for a moment, stroking his beard. "And we've done very little to change it," he said. "Seeing what a burlesque and sham the boat is, but still not daring to rock it. Bless the ones who are starting to rock it now." He crossed his legs and looked at his black boatlike shoes. "I was fired for being gay. Did you know that?"

James put his glass down, grasped his pipe, and stood with a curious pinched expression on his face. He breathed heavily once, twice . . . whipped out a handkerchief and sneezed explosively into it, his entire body convulsed by the effort. He was suddenly sweating. He did not want to hear this.

"No, you couldn't have known it. Before I was hired at Calistoga, when I was at the other place."

"You said you had resigned," James wheezed.

"Of course I said I'd resigned. In 1960 that was what you said. I wasn't ready to tell you or anyone the real reasons." He sat back with a heavy sigh. "So, ten years after McCarthy, fifteen after Hitler's Germany. I keep trying to put this into some historical perspective, you see, to try to understand it. Nineteen hundred and sixty. I was thirty-seven. I'd been at the college for three years. I thought I had friends there and I'd been told that I was the best choral director they'd had in years."

James sat down opposite his brother, his face pale.

"There was an organist at the college who was a damned good musician but what nervous people call indiscreet. He was rather exaggerated, you know, but perfectly friendly and more than competent. Why they ever hired him I'll never know, because suddenly I was called into an emergency department meeting. He wasn't there, of course, this all being secret: the married males club, with me as the exception. So there they were, discussing how to get rid of him. It had somehow become known that he was queer, as they said. And so they decided simply not to renew his contract for the following year and suggested to him that he resign immediately. How this had become known about him they wouldn't say, only hint, so my guess is that it was an anonymous letter."

"An anonymous letter," James said.

"I was outraged. And also terrified, because they were also talking about *me*, if only they'd known it. I was queer too, only I was not only discreet, but celibate. This was all being done behind the fellow's back with no chance for him to defend himself. There were no substantiated charges, there was no evidence, and even if there had been, what difference did it make if the guy was a good organist?

"I sat there . . . my heart pounding, wondering how I could defend him. And finally one of them made a remark, something about homosexuality being a disease—and this from a man I myself would've thought was a closet case—and Jesus, you know, I just blew up. I called them a pack of witch-hunters. I defended the guy professionally and as a musician. I said it was none of our business what he did when he wasn't at work, and that there was no way to connect homosexuality with job performance. I just let out everything I could without saying that I was myself gay. And of course that was what their hysteria immediately did. Suddenly I was no longer one of them. And Jesus, Jim, I was glad to realize that I wasn't. That was another signpost in my life."

"So how did they get you?" James asked.

"The same trick they wanted to use on him. They didn't renew my contract. When I asked them why, they made a lame excuse, made up some lies, said I hadn't been exactly what they had been looking for in a choral director. There was no way I could fight it, or the other guy either. Neither of us had tenure. It was their move all the way; their way to abuse their power. Nothing about my being gay was mentioned, of course. It didn't need to be. It was completely understood. We both had to be drummed out of the married males' mutual protection league.

"And in the crazy way that things work," Loren said, "I've never had a better thing happen to me as far as being a musician goes, or as far as being a human being goes. It was humiliating, and I was scared—shit, I was terrified. But I was lucky, too. Of course I didn't know what sort of recommendation they'd give me, what sort of nonsense and lies they'd make up. Anything's possible with a group of men like that huddling together and deciding things in secret. At Calistoga many of my colleagues may be stranded in the nineteenth century musically, but personally they're not the same."

"How do you know?" James asked. "Have you tried them?"

"One or two. The ones I like. I've gotten much better at being me."

"This house—" James said suddenly, nervously, drawing vigorously on his unlit pipe, his eyes scanning the room. It had some connection to what Loren was telling him, but he could not define it.

"You can have it, I told you," said Loren. "This house to me is just another lie. A lie we grew up with and the lie we were supposed to believe was somehow superior to any other way of life. This house . . . I'll tell you, this house is two strangers living together under the obvious illusion that marriage is all that's possible or desirable in life. Two people growing to hate one another because of the strain of the lie. This house is mother being afraid to be German and being afraid of her husband, and it's father being afraid of me because I loved music, being afraid of what that meant, being afraid of what his neighbors would think, being afraid to show any affection or emotion because it wasn't masculine. This house is nothing but fears and lies to me and I don't want anything to do with it."

"Four strangers," James said. "You were always a stranger to me."

"Five strangers. You made Daniel into a stranger here. This old lying fearful house. The lie could've been broken when Daniel lived here with you. Why wouldn't you let it?"

"Don't sit there like some goddamned poetic sage and tell me what I've done wrong with *my* life!" James said hotly, instantly on the defensive. "I know I haven't been good with my emotions—they embarrass me and always have. Don't you think that I know that I'm no good at loving? Don't you think it's been hell knowing how clumsy and ill-prepared for it I was? And what about you? Celibate you? What the hell do you really know about any of it?"

Surprised, Loren floundered in his chair. "I've been in love twice in my life," he said. "Once with Peter and once with a student who—left me. I never told either of them. And that was one of my demons—two of them, rather. Never speaking out, bottling up my heart. It was probably fear, I suspect it was. So when I saw how it was possible, and saw how you were denying it—"

"All that stuff he'd go on about . . . emotions and being unconscious in love. It's all very easy to say, but the world doesn't allow it. Being unself-conscious would for me have to be a conscious effort, and that invalidates it."

This long strange journey with ourselves, Loren thought.

Thinking we know the crannies and cupboards and discovering that they are false depths. We are thrown an anchor here and there, but even then we are carried on. All the movings and all the endings, the turning of years within the brain and the body. Before we can move on, live on, we have to shed the dragging, drowning past. What is there to comprehend, finally, but that it is all a continual flow?

"I want you to go back to Daniel," he said. "Because I know that you want him back. I want you to do what you want to do but can't."

"You want me to do what you've never dared to do yourself."

"Yes," Loren said. "That too."

James stooped with the force of a tremendous sneeze. "Even if I wanted him back he wouldn't come."

"You've decided that. It makes it easier for you to remain frozen."

"Don't you know that he's fucking your fucking ex-lover right now?" James shouted. "He's with Puckett. He went to Germany to be with him. With Puckett!" he cried, and stood for a moment wondering if tears were finally going to come. They blurred his vision but did not fall.

"I know," Loren said calmly. "Daniel wrote me. But Puckett will never be more than temporary for anybody. That's just how he is. People don't fit into his career. Daniel knows that. Puckett's a kind of cushion for Daniel. It's not serious."

"Was all of this in his letter?"

"Some of it, a lot of it between the lines. He said he had to be away, had to be a coward for a while. Couldn't stay here."

"I won't coerce him," James said. Quietly, unexpectedly, he began to cry. "I couldn't. He's made up his mind."

"You've made up his mind. There's a difference."

"I do not coerce people," James insisted. "Everyone must take responsibility for his own decisions."

"Except when those decisions are made because of fear and inhibitions. Decisions, to mean anything, have to be made in freedom, in the clear air."

"Don't polemicize, I'm too tired."

"Did you once ask him to stay?"

"Damn it, it's none of your business."

"What the hell did you do? Sit there and listen to him and then watch him pack and not say a word?"

"Yes, yes, more or less. I couldn't disagree with anything he said. I was hurt and I confess I hadn't expected it, but he had made his decision and I respected it." His eyes became slits and his chest filled. "Except for—for—" After three sneezes he paused on the brink of a fourth long enough to wheeze, "—for his going to Puckett. Why did he tell me that?"

Loren waited for the last sneeze before saying, "Because that's where he was going."

He sat, James stood, neither spoke until James said, "Let's not talk about this anymore tonight. I'm too tired. Not that I'll sleep."

Loren got up and put a hand on his brother's shoulder, squeezing it, before he shuffled off towards the stairs. He could sleep now. Sleep had returned to him. "Good night."

"Yes," James said, standing by the fire.

I've really worked him up, Loren thought.

"Loren? I am—glad. About this. About talking to you, I mean. I haven't had anyone I could talk to. Tell things. They build up, you know?"

"I know."

The wind blew but a curious silence had fallen through the house. A thick gray-green light, the light of lush wet summers, of grass and trees and cloud-thick Oregon skies, gave the rooms a slightly sinister look. James, in his dream, was

wandering through the house, opening doors, peering into one
room after another. In every room there was a window and he
was compelled to look out into the blowing silence, seeing the
trees wave and bend, seeing the dark sky, hearing nothing. All
sound was dead.

Daniel was in the bedroom of James' parents, sitting in a
chair in the corner, naked, a spade beside him. James stared,
hungry for his body. He entered the room and let Daniel undress him. They lay down on his parents' bed and began to
make love.

The door opened and his parents entered. James was in a
panic and tried to hide Daniel under the blankets. His parents
sat down on the side of the bed and looked at him. James began
to jabber—he had a voice and he tried to apologize to them for
what he had done, tried to explain to them what he was doing.
But his words were incoherent and the more he struggled to
enunciate or express himself, the more garbled and terrible
and absurd the words became. His mother and father looked at
him, their faces kind and blank. They understood nothing.
They rose and left the room. James was sweating profusely. He
remembered Daniel and pulled the blankets back. Daniel was
dead. He had suffocated.

James wandered through the house crying, lamenting.
His sorrow was powerful, intense. Outside, the silent wind
blew and blew. James met Tilda and she gave him a portrait of
Daniel which she had just finished. The paint was still wet.
James looked closer. The flowers were real, smelled fresh.
"Yes," Tilda said, "but he is dead. You can peel off his face, if
you wish. You can hang it up to kiss it, or put it on your own
face."

James was now in a room by himself. Outside, the silent
wind blew and blew. The thick gray-green light stalled in the
window, leaving most of the room black. James approached the
casket where Daniel lay. Tilda had arranged an intricate three-
dimensional plan of the gardens on either side of him. James

looked tenderly into the casket. His mother was lying there. She shifted, obviously asleep.

James was terrified. He looked over and saw Daniel outside, a frightened look on his face. James ran to the window but could not hear what Daniel was saying. The glass was too thick. Daniel rapped frantically on the glass, pointing towards the sky, the gardens, James could not tell which. He motioned for James to open the window, quickly, quickly, but James' arms were so heavy he could hardly lift them. And weak. He had no strength to turn the latch or pull the window up. Daniel began to beat on the glass, pound on it, his face awful to look at, filled with horror and panic.

James now saw people emerge from the gardens, men wearing black suits and horn-rimmed glasses. He understood that they were after Daniel, who was also somehow Loren. A drenching rain began to fall. Daniel pleaded to be let in through the window, pounding and beating on the glass, as the men in black suits moved closer. They had weapons of some kind, ropes or lassoes. But James' arms were still so weak, so helpless.

Suddenly James was shoved out of the way by his father, who had a tool kit, and proceeded to work on the window. James was not certain if his father was trying to open the window or make it even more difficult to open. "That's wrong, that's wrong," he tried to say, but the words were lost in his throat.

And then James' mother was there, and his father moved aside. She pointed to a secret latch, undid it, and pulled up the window. A sharp, fragrant, summer-wet wind roared into the room. James, his mother, his father, all reached out to pull Daniel into the room. Daniel's feet had been lassoed by the men in black suits and they tugged from outside. With a sudden jerk, Daniel flew from James' and his parents' hands and was dragged across the wet grass by the men, dragged into the gardens like a victim to be sacrificed.

In a wet, steaming jungle-place which thrived in a mysterious fertile twilight, James was searching, searching. Hot
raindrops fell from the leaves. James was sweating, clammy,
forever pushing aside thick growths obscuring the path.
Through a tangle of vines he saw his mother, with her gardening basket on her arm. She began to speak to him in a language
James could not understand, but which he knew to be German.
He felt a kind of calm happiness to hear her and know she was
near, also searching.

"Oh," she said, and now he could understand her. "Here
is his heart."

James pushed his way through the vines, towards his
mother.

She was standing with a small object in her hand. It
looked to James like a bird. "See?" she said, showing him.
"Here is his heart."

James asked, thrilled with fright, if it was still alive.

His mother put her ear to it. "Yes," she said. "Yes, it is
still alive. Will you hold it?"

James took the small strange thing in his hands. It was
very hot.

"You may keep it," his mother said.

A great relief spread through James. He felt the heat of
the heart warming his arms, his legs, his entire body. Together
they stood and looked tenderly at Daniel's heart, cupped there
in James' hand, in the garden.

"I got you this ticket for the opera tonight, *Schatz*," Puckett
said at lunch. They were in a restaurant on the Kurfürsten-
damm. "*Fidelio*."

Daniel noticed him eyeing and then smiling at a young
man sitting a few tables away and laughed to himself as he stirred his coffee.

"And what is so amusing?" Puckett asked. "Why the smirk after days of gloom?"

"I'm not smirking, I'm smiling," Daniel said. He laughed out loud. "How will you make a rendezvous?"

Puckett looked again at the German man, who nodded. "Yes, attractive, no? I've seen him before—"

"Even if you haven't, that's a good line to use when you introduce yourself."

"Yes, but there's just one thing, *Schatz*," Puckett said. "What?"

"He's interested in you—not me."

"Don't be absurd," Daniel said, but turned surreptitiously to look. The German smiled at him and nodded again.

"Are you going to do anything about it?" Puckett asked. "Aren't you going to at least *nod*?"

"No," Daniel said, laughing again.

"You know, *Schatz*," Puckett gave Daniel's hand a tap. "Don't you think it would be better if you began to follow up on this sort of opportunity?"

"I've never been good at it. I mean in the casual, 'Hello, how are you, let's fuck' manner."

"That's how it was with me, wasn't it?" Puckett said. "Sex, nothing but good old sex, that's what we both sensed and wanted."

"I was also attracted to your mind," Daniel said.

"My mind?" Puckett said, a note of disbelief in his voice. He was interrupted by two women in mink coats who approached the table and began speaking to him in German. Puckett, perfect gentleman, rose and shook their hands. A short conversation followed, all smiles and laughter. He signed autographs for them and, leaving a lingering trail of perfume, they were gone. There was pleasure, even happiness, in Puckett's face as he sat down again. "My mind," he said. "I thought you didn't like my mind very much."

"I never said that. I don't agree with you half the time, but that doesn't mean that I don't like your mind."

"You make me sound like a specimen," Puckett said.

"An attraction of brains, is that so odd? It makes the sexual side of it that much more exciting. At least to me. People stay together because of brains, not bodies."

"If they stay together at all. Christ, Daniel, you simply cannot see anything as temporary. Everything is so goddamned eternal with you. The world's not like that anymore, baby. Everything is temporary now."

"Love never sees itself as temporary. That's what makes it so peculiar. Haven't you ever been in love?"

Puckett looked at him. "Once, yes. I was in love with Loren. When I was his student. And for a long time afterwards too, I suppose. But he pushed me out of the nest by arranging for me to come to Germany. We never had sex. I wanted to, but we never did."

"Did you ever tell him? Did you ever come out and say, 'Loren, I love you'?"

"No. I was different then. Perhaps I wasn't. It doesn't matter, it's over now." With that he closed the subject. "About this ticket for the opera tonight. I'm going to be busy, but I wanted you to see it." He felt in his coat pocket for the ticket. "Promise me you'll go."

Daniel took the ticket. "You want the apartment for private intrigues?"

"Yes, yes. But look, *Schatz*, it's important that you go."

"All right, I'll go and cry my eyes out at another tragic ending."

"But *Fidelio* has a happy ending," Puckett said.

"I've never seen it," Daniel said. "Well, even happy endings can make me cry."

* * * * * * *

The weather broke that day. The stalled gray sky and dull penetrating chill of Berlin cracked under the force of a fresh and awakening wind. All afternoon the sky was in motion, new cloud formations joining, breaking, sailing on, grand and mysterious in the pale November blue.

On the streets of Berlin people were pushed along by it. The scenery changed every minute, as if there were an uproar behind the curtains. It showered, it blew, the sun was out, a thin mist softened the outlines of buildings. Umbrellas were blown inside-out and as the owner cursed and struggled the sun came out to poke him in the eye. Canvas awnings flapped, paper skittered, the trees moved in a sea of wind.

Berliners were seen staring dreamily from shop and apartment windows, as if they wanted to be outside, where cheeks were reddened and hats flew off. In the *Tiergarten* the animals stopped prowling the endless routine of their concrete domains, stood with heads up, sniffing. The lions roared, an elephant trumpeted, exotic birds shrieked and hopped in the aviary. The hippopotami surfaced, opened their fleshy pink and grey mouths, and bellowed. Doors blew open, doors blew shut. The wind was life.

And Daniel felt alive, felt all the secrets, all the strange, illiterate, overwhelming sensations, joy and sorrow, hope and hopelessness, at once and together. When Puckett went off to his fencing lesson with the handsome Hungarian, that to be followed by another visit to his teacher, Frau Vogelkind-Schneiderhasten, that to be followed by a meeting with his agent, and that to be followed by the study of a new role, Siegmund in *Die Walküre*, Daniel set off for his walk. It was a farewell walk to Berlin, which he was leaving the next morning.

That, he decided, was one of the reasons why Puckett had arranged for him to attend the opera that evening. There would be less chance for an impulsive, emotional scene; no romantic lingering over goodbyes. It seemed unlikely that they would ever see one another again.

But they did, that evening, before Daniel left for the opera house. He was dressing slowly, dreamily, going often to the window to look out. Under a black, clear sky he could see the trees in the *Grünewald* moving in a kind of solemn, windy dance. The stars pressed hard brilliant imprints into the sheen, as if some grunting German *Putzfrau* had been hard at work scrubbing and buffing clean the entire floor of heaven.

What was there about a wind that could move him so? He felt as if he were going out to meet a lover, one familiar but always new. There was the moon, bright as it rarely was, making its processional through the sky—the ancient moon seen by anyone who cared to look, Communist or Capitalist, on both sides of the Wall.

He was staring out the window with his arms crossed when Puckett came in and joined him there. He wrapped his arms around Daniel from behind and pressed close to him.

"You smell like the wind," Daniel said.

"I had a bit of a walk. You're on your way to the opera I see."

"Yes. And I've packed my suitcase and hidden it in the armoire so that your amour of the evening won't see it. And afterwards I'll go to a cafe on the Ku-Damm and drink a coffee and dally."

"Look, *Schatz,* as the fencing master said to me today, maybe it is that we don't see you no longer again." Daniel's hands tightened on his arms. "And to tell the truth, I don't have anything to say."

"I don't either," Daniel said, turning to him. "It's not like an opera, is it?"

"I'll miss you, *Schatz.* Does that surprise you? But I predict you'll fall in love again very soon and be able to grub around in the dirt of those gardens you're so crazy about. Now we'll kiss once and you'll be off to hear Beethoven, and in the morning a taxi will take you to the airport—"

"No, I'm taking the bus, it's cheaper."

"All right, the bus. Let's close up our chapter now so that tomorrow morning will be easier. And then you'd better hurry or you'll miss the curtain."

The dull indistinct roar of an opera house filled with people; a downpour of sound. Voices waiting to hear voices. Daniel flipped through the program. He remembered an evening at Francis Turner's house, the night he first met James. A ridiculous and overwhelming swell of tenderness and sorrow made him gulp down a breath. He saw James sitting there in Francis' house, a handsome, intriguing stranger as bored as he was with the superabundance of vocalizing that Francis and Dobbin found so thrilling. We didn't meet in the real world at all, he thought.

The houselights went down, the conductor was applauded, the overture began. During the two intermissions Daniel promenaded with the rest of the well-dressed Germans. They stared at his clothes and shoes as they sipped from plastic goblets of champagne and downed liters of beer.

The third act was preceded by the Leonora Overture. During it, a person who had come in the dark and taken the empty seat three down from Daniel suddenly shifted his position and extracted a handkerchief from his pocket, trying to muffle a sneeze.

Sneezes can be as distinctive as fingerprints, and hearing this one startled Daniel. He kept himself from looking, however, so as not to appear rude. But his heart began to race when the sneeze came again, and this time he quickly turned.

There, three seats away, sat James, his eyes looking out apologetically, surprisedly, nervously, from above his handkerchief.

A strange throat-clearing sound rose in Daniel's throat and he turned his burning, disbelieving face back towards the stage.

When he turned again, the two people sitting between him and James shot forbidding glances in his direction. On the other side of them, James shyly lowered the handkerchief, staring back intently, until in a sudden spasm he leaned back, shut his eyes, raised the handkerchief.

This time the two people looked furiously at James, heaving their outraged bodies in their seats and making shaming noises with their tongues. The overture played on. James held his position until he had conquered the sneeze. The two people were shocked when James suddenly reached across them and took Daniel's hand.

James gave a tug. Daniel stood. Holding hands they set the entire first balcony in an uproar as they excused themselves, laughing and treading on toes that bitterly refused to move and make their departure easier. The orchestra played on with all the force and discipline the conductor could muster. They might have been playing for the two men who stood looking at one another in the hallway of the opera house, the two men who embraced, kissed and hurried out into the windy Berlin night.

Spring

1981

"Daniel? Telephone, it's Tilda. Daniel?" James stepped out from the terrace doors and called into the garden. He knew Daniel was working somewhere to prepare a bed for some early seeds.

Thick spring clouds moved slowly, uncertainly, afloat in wonder, through a pale sky. The earliest cherry trees were popped with blossoms and the camellias and Japanese quince offered bold colors to the eye. Crocus, snowdrops and primroses rang in bright clumps. The gardens otherwise had a tense, impatient look to them, as if they were hungry to blossom.

"Daniel? Telephone!"

James cupped his hands to his mouth to be heard over the wind. It felt like cold silk on his face. Daniel particularly enjoyed these windy days of earliest spring. He had not been well of late, James knew, but he refused to talk about it.

Calling once more, James jogged into the garden and down the central gravel path. Turning right, he wound around behind a tall hedge of laurel. There he saw Daniel lying on his back on the soilbed he had been preparing. For a black terrifying moment James was certain that he was dead. He whispered Daniel's name sharply under his breath and ran to him, ran to the life stretched there, the face as white as the bone-meal spilling from its sack behind him. He ran to the body of the man he loved, the man who had shared his life for so long, the person he had seen pass through the altering years.

The wind had a desolate, distant, unbearably stupid sound as James raced to him. And that was the beginning of a new season, when a step had been taken towards death, the harvest.

Down the center path at a creeping pace two men walk at twilight.

One has been terribly ill, beaten and starved by whatever disease tyrannizes his body. It is not easy to look at him, as the other man is doing. James has one arm supportively around Daniel's fleshless waist. With his other he holds one of the cold, damp, skeletal hands.

"Has it ever occurred to you," Daniel whispers hoarsely, "that we must look as though we're doing some strange dance when we walk like this? A schottisch maybe?"

Spring is at its fullest, richest climax these days, these glorious sweet twilights. The fruit trees are heavy with clouds of white and pink blossom. Daffodils, tulips, iris, daisies, candytuft, scented stock and wallflowers, all the earliest flowers are out in abundance, beginning to fill in the year-long patchwork quilt of color, scent and shape that are the gardens. Dark sweet fragrances hover in the air. The songs of the birds drop like liquid from the trees.

"There's a chill tonight," James says. "Aren't you uncomfortable?"

"A chill, a chill." Daniel is impatient. "After being in that bed all day, in half a stupor—don't forget to cut back the perennials there." He stops for a moment, exhausted. "The old roses and herbs could be our goal tonight, don't you think? Oof, just a bit slower."

They pass Sylvie's grave, covered with a large bush of purple-flowered rosemary.

"Can you smell the stocks?" Daniel asks. "Even I can smell them. I tell you, all my senses seem to be honed sharp when I come out after being in all day. Remember that the tuberoses have to be dug up and stored during the winter. Ah, there's so damned much to do. Is that Vertumnus already?"

"He has moss growing in his hand," James says. "You know what that means."

Daniel laughs, but it's a changed laugh, a weakened laugh. "Too much jerking off when no one's around to see."

They sit on a stone bench facing the Roman god of gardens.

"I love this spot," Daniel says. "Just uncut grass and water in a stone basin and old Vertumnus." He is silent for a moment. "Those lines of Emily Dickinson: 'that bareheaded life under the grass worries one like a wasp.' " James looks away. "Don't—don't. Try not to because then I will and damn it I'm too weak to cry. I can't walk and weep at the same time."

"I can't help it," James says, wiping his nose. Eyes closed, he turns to take his lover in his arms, his head held tight against the bony chest. He hears the loud rapid hammering of a heart, the noise of life.

"Maybe I shouldn't say such things," says Daniel, "but I feel as if I have to—'to drive the awe away,' as Emily would say. Honesty is about all I've got left. And we can't pretend it isn't there, or rather here, in me." He holds James tighter in his weak cold arms. "I'm sorry it's so difficult, this dying."

"Don't say that. I know I'm weak."

With a loud sniff, Daniel lifts his head. "James, we're turning into drivel." They look shyly at one another, both faces miserable but Daniel's frightening. His eyes are sunk back in dark, feverish, death-licked hollows. They laugh to steady themselves. "I do want you to know that my life has been almost everything it could be. And that's because of you. Because you came to me. Remember that crazy night in Berlin?"

"Ten years ago. I don't think I could forget it," James says.

"It was a turning point. Love winning instead of letting itself lose. Even if there have been rough spots since then."

"Yes," James says.

They sit without speaking, holding one another as the twilight eases itself into darkness.

"These gardens have made me very happy too," Daniel says. He wonders for a moment if he should tell James that the first day he looked out into the gardens he saw a dead woman with a basket of roses on her arm. He decides not to. "It's terrible and mysterious," he whispers, "this waiting. I've always jabbered about how important feeling is, and here I am faced with the culmination of all feeling. Good God, what a strange strange thing a mind is, and what a strange strange thing a self is. And life. You say, 'I've lived—this is my life' and yet you don't understand what it is, it remains perpetually incomprehensible. Except for this—a garden—the old cycles—the ancient seasons. This comes back every year to remind you of what you still have and what you've lost and what you're losing."

James looks at him, trying to understand what that self called Daniel is, how that rich, generous life that is Daniel's can be destroyed this way by a brutal, unreasoning, unknown and incurable disease. The bitter irony of death, coming unwanted to someone always so full of life. He beats down the panic that jumps hot into his own brain and body many times a day; he beats down the terror that rattles his throat and blurs his vision. He tries simply to understand the peculiar evolution that enables a brain to stand back, prepare, and wonder at its own demise.

"I have to tell you some of the things that go through my mind," Daniel says. "It makes me feel less lonely. Because all around you everything goes on its merry way. The birds keep singing, and the flowers bloom. You suddenly know that they will, even when you're not here to appreciate them. It makes me feel very tiny, almost ludicrous. Does that make sense? It's a fight sometimes to feel sense in anything. It's not exactly that I'm afraid, because at times I feel connected, absolutely connected, with everything, and there's no fear in that. Dying's a part of it all. Ah, I can't tell you what I mean. Just that all the miserable and ridiculous systems that men concoct to keep themselves miserable and ridiculous are so wrong. Unnecessary. If you're connected to the world, to the earth, to a garden, you don't concoct artificial systems. You don't have to. You can just let yourself be a part of it. Oof, that last medication is starting to kick in. Things are a little blurry."

James stands to help him up.

"I don't want to get back in yet," Daniel says. "Not just yet."

James crouches before him. "I love you so much."

"I know. That's what's most important to me now."

Seated on the stone bench, they embrace again.

Myths are always tempting. They make things understandable in the beginning and the end, solve problems by fictional example, and give people vicarious hope and endurance to face the age-old sorrows of life, the passing of life, the conclusion of living.

When James was a boy he was taught that dying was really rather pretty. In colored pictures he saw how easy it was. Solemn, radiant angels took a corner of your soul and pulled it loose from your limp, smiling body. You didn't really change at all. There were fat-cheeked cherub heads popping out from banks of clouds overhead, watching with apparent delight, and the solemn angels flew away with you to Paradise, provided, of course, that you had died in a state of grace. There, in Paradise, you met The Heavenly Royalty seated on their thrones with the Holy Ghost hovering above them.

What was so bad about the pretty colored pictures of graceful dying? That they had no application to the way things really were? But, then, what does a child know of grief, or of the pain to come?

Daniel was dead. He who had so much life no longer lived. James had buried his ashes in the garden, near a favorite old-fashioned rose which Daniel himself had chosen.

What was death? Going beyond the convenient and simplistic conceptions, what did you have to help your understanding, your continuing consciousness of it all? It seemed more mysterious, perhaps more meaningful (if it had any meaning at all) when you simply tried to think of nothing—of the great airy spacious blankness left when human life was over.

For whom do we grieve, after all, if not for ourselves? The dead have no ears to hear us. For them it is over. It is nothing. Their season is past.

James mostly walks alone in the gardens now. Sometimes Tilda or another friend is on his arm. They talk so quietly when they talk at all.

The gardens, continuing, lend themselves to a kind of remembering, and seem themselves to be doing the same.

James has never had very much imagination, but is it imagination or simply a typical phenomenon of a mind still in love? There are times when Daniel seems not gone at all. That he is, is still incomprehensible. Perhaps that explains it. For walking down certain of Daniel's favorite paths, there are moments when James feels he is approaching a presence, though he sees and hears nothing.

What is it? Nothing frightening. Familiar, rather, and comfortable. Perhaps only the habits of thinking and expectation, for how many times had he walked out here not knowing exactly where Daniel was, but knowing that he was somewhere?

His analytical machinery was useless and jammed when confronted with death. He couldn't understand it if he tried. There was now nothing, where once there had been a great loving force. He still felt the power of it keening in his heart.

Light is different to his eyes now. He looks forward to twilight and the last light of the day. That is when he likes to stroll through the gardens. Around him the flowers bloom, the trees have leaves, the vegetables mature to ripeness. Hidden birds sing singly, here, there: deep, simple summations of the day and the coming night.